P9-CEG-036

Disney
CHILLS

PART OF YOUR
NIGHTMARE

DISNEY CHILLS

PART OF YOUR NIGHTMARE

Disney PRESS

Los Angeles · New York

Copyright © 2020 Disney Enterprises, Inc.
Illustrations by Jeffrey Thomas © Disney Enterprises, Inc.
Design by Lindsay Broderick

All rights reserved. Published by Disney Press, an imprint of
Buena Vista Books, Inc. No part of this book may be reproduced or
transmitted in any form or by any means, electronic or mechanical,
including photocopying, recording, or by any information storage and
retrieval system, without written permission from the publisher.
For information address Disney Press, 1200 Grand Central Avenue,
Glendale, California 91201.

Printed in the United States of America
First Paperback Edition, July 2020
1 3 5 7 9 10 8 6 4 2
FAC-025438-20143

Library of Congress Control Number: 2020930908
ISBN 978-1-368-04825-5

For more Disney Press fun, visit www.disneybooks.com

If you purchased this book without a cover, you should be
aware that this book is stolen property. It was reported
as "unsold and destroyed" to the publisher, and
neither the author nor the publisher has received
any payment for this "stripped" book.

SUSTAINABLE
FORESTRY
INITIATIVE

Certified Sourcing

www.sfiprogram.org
SFI-01054

The SFI label applies to the text stock

The dreams that you
FEAR will come true.

1

UNDER THE SEA

Cold water enveloped Shelly as she plunged.

She spiraled down through what appeared to be tangles of kelp. What was happening to her? Where was she going? Finally, she somersaulted to a stop in a dim underwater cavern.

She began to swim, holding her breath, not sure where she was going, just knowing she needed to find an exit, to find air. But seaweed snagged at her ankles, trapping her.

"Leave here . . . turn back!" came a tiny, pained voice as clear as day, even that far underwater.

Shelly looked down and saw *faces* on the seaweed. And

with her heart racing and air running out, she realized it wasn't seaweed at all, but withered gray life-forms with sallow eyes and gaping, contorted mouths. They were nothing she had ever studied or seen in the aquarium. They couldn't be talking to her, though. She must have imagined it.

A current gripped her and sucked her down.

She tried to swim against it, but it was too strong. Her lungs ached, fit to burst.

Suddenly, an enormous crystal ball clamped around her, and her mouth opened in a silent scream. But then the water drained from the enclosure, and she was able to breathe, though she spluttered and spat and pounded her fists on the curved crystal.

"Help! Let me out!" she yelled. Everything looked distorted through the glass. She could barely make out the underwater cavern. Glass bottles lined the rough-hewn walls, and there were glowing anemones and the eyes of those . . . *things*. She gasped as something huge, bulbous, and black swam past her. *What was that?*

"Lose something, dear?" The same deep, rich voice

she'd heard in her little brother's bedroom emanated from the shadowy corner of the cavern. "So coy!" A black tentacle shot out of the gloom and rapped on the glass. Shelly cowered, fear gripping her.

"Wh-what do you want?" she gasped.

THREE DAYS EARLIER . . .

2
#STRAWSSUCK

"**C**ircle up and pay attention, students!"

Mr. Aquino attempted to corral his class, a rowdy group of sixth graders from Triton Bay Middle School, as they gathered around the main aquarium exhibit. When the chatter quieted only a little, he raised his voice again. "Now, who can tell me what *this* marine animal is called?" he said, pointing to a large graceful creature paddling through the rippling blue water.

Before Shelly could stop herself, she stuck up her hand. "Leatherback sea turtle."

"Very good, Shelly," Mr. Aquino said. "Now, why do sea turtles eat plastic bags?"

"'Cuz they're dumb fish!" Normie Watson said, prompting snickering.

"Actually, they're not *fish*—they're *reptiles*," Mr. Aquino said with a disapproving frown. "And they're *not* dumb. They're actually very smart! Now . . . anybody else?"

Shelly was secretly glad that he'd shut Normie down. *Serves him right.* She watched the sea turtle drift past the sunken pirate ship and treasure chest that decorated the faux-undersea environment. It wheeled around a rusty, barnacled trident, the centerpiece of the exhibit, which stuck out from the bright white sand. Suddenly, a huge reef shark swam behind Mr. Aquino.

"Watch out!" Normie yelped, pointing to its huge jaws, filled with jagged teeth. Gasps and nervous giggles rang out. "Megalodon just tried to chomp Mr. Aquino's head!" he said.

As if anything could swim through the glass, Shelly thought. She thrust up her hand again, since no one had answered their teacher's question yet, and Mr. Aquino pointed at her.

"Because sea turtles mistake plastic bags for jellyfish, their main food source," she said.

"Correct again, Shelly," Mr. Aquino said, flashing her a smile while her classmates groaned.

Shelly's new best friend, Kendall, shot her a look and mouthed one word: *Nerd.* Attina and Alana—the twins who rounded out their friend group—giggled at Shelly. Kendall had long blond hair that swooped around her shoulders like it was out of a shampoo commercial and blue-green eyes the color of the sea. The twins were identical, with curly auburn hair in a stylish asymmetrical bob and brown eyes. All three girls were dressed the same, in designer athleisure clothes from Ever After Boutique in downtown Triton Bay, the quaint seaside city where they lived. The trio also slurped iced lattes from disposable plastic cups with two plastic straws *each*. Shelly's cheeks burned with embarrassment.

I shouldn't have kept raising my hand, Shelly thought. It was a hard instinct to fight.

Science nerds were more revolting than rotting fish to the popular kids. She'd had to change schools at the beginning of the school year, when her mother moved her and her little brother, Dawson, from their big old house by the ocean to the townhouse in the complex on the edge of the canals, and it had taken her many long months to make new friends.

One glorious day, Kendall had invited Shelly to sit with her group at lunch. Shelly had become fast friends with the three of them after that. *Nothing* was going to ruin Shelly's happiness about that friendship, including her father leaving their house and moving into the weird dingy apartment with the stained carpets that always smelled like greasy delivery food, and her brother's goldfish, Mr. Bubbles, going belly-up and getting flushed down the toilet the past week. *Nothing* was worse than having no friends.

"Nice job, Shelly," Mr. Aquino said with a wink, snapping her out of her thoughts.

"*Nice job, Shelly,*" Normie mocked. "*Of course* she knows everything about fish."

Everyone knew that Shelly's parents owned the Triton Bay Aquarium. A year earlier, she and her little brother used to love going to work with their parents on the weekends, following their mother around while she managed the feeding schedules and directed the staffers, or hanging with their father in the office while he handled the bills and dealt with guest relations.

But the days of both her parents being at the aquarium at the same time had passed.

Shelly followed as Mr. Aquino led the class to the next tank on the tour. Shelly caught sight of her reflection in the tank's clear barrier. She had long, curly dark hair streaked with blond highlights from all the time she spent on the aquarium's outdoor sundeck feeding the dolphins. Her eyebrows and eyes were darker brown than her sun-kissed skin. Her favorite thing about her appearance was her long, strong legs, which helped her swim fast.

Sunlight filtered through the water, casting strange shadows onto her classmates. She didn't need to look at the illustrated placard to know what this exhibit housed: spiny lobsters, stingrays, barracuda, and garden eels. The lobsters, looking like giant red insects waving their antennas, lumbered around the bottom of the tank filled with coral reef and sea sponges.

Mr. Aquino held up a white plastic straw. "Now, can someone tell me what *this* is?"

They all stifled their laughter at the easy question. All except for Shelly, who prevented her arm from rising. She wasn't going to risk Kendall calling her a nerd again.

"Uhhh, I'm pretty sure that's a straw," said Normie. "Do I get extra credit now?"

The class broke into laughter.

Our sea sponges *here are smarter than Normie,* Shelly thought with a head shake.

"It's not just *any* straw," Mr. Aquino replied, ignoring Normie's request. He slipped into his full-on enthusiastic-teacher mode, waving the straw around. "It's a plastic straw I found on the beach this morning." He paused for dramatic effect. "Did you know that ninety percent of seabirds and fifty percent of sea turtles have been found to have plastic in their stomachs?"

Shelly felt a lump form in her throat. She *did* know. How could she not? She used to be the head of the Kids Care Conservation Club at the aquarium. Earlier that year, she had spoken to Mr. Aquino about starting a chapter at school. That was before she became friends with Kendall.

"This straw looks harmless enough," Mr. Aquino

went on, gesturing to the exhibit, where a smiling sting-ray drifted serenely behind the glass. "But it's no laughing matter. This little straw could kill an endangered animal like that turtle—or *poison* our precious oceans."

"Death by *killer* straws," Kendall murmured, shaking her iced latte with its two straws at Attina and Alana. "Anything but the Killer Straws!" she added, flicking the tops of the straws.

Attina and Alana giggled at her quip and sipped from their own iced lattes.

Shelly cringed, feeling bad for Mr. Aquino.

Her teacher gave up. "All right, I'll give you two options—dolphin exhibit or gift shop."

They all yelled, "Gift shop!" at the top of their lungs.

Shelly kept her mouth shut. She wanted to visit the dolphins—watch the feeders toss fish to Sassy and Salty and maybe even dip her hand into the open-air tank and pet Lil' Mermy, the youngest dolphin in the pod. But it would just have to wait for another time.

Fit in at all costs, she told herself as she sidled up to her new friends.

"Please," Kendall said to her posse, then loudly slurped

13

her iced latte through its two straws. "First no more plastic bags, and now they want to take away my straws? No thanks."

"For realz," Attina chimed in, fiddling with her sparkly headband, which perfectly matched her sister's, though Attina's was pink and Alana's was blue. "Who cares about boring old fish, anyway?"

"Hashtag BTD," Alana added. "Bored to death." She drank from her iced latte.

The three girls turned to Shelly expectantly, each sipping from her drink.

"Right . . . so boring," Shelly mumbled, forcing out the opposite of what she actually felt.

"Totally," said Kendall with a smile. "Shells, we love how you're such a know-it-all."

Alana and Attina tittered at her remark.

Shelly didn't know how to take it, so she simply smiled. "Thanks, I think," she said.

The girls began to trail behind the rest of the class, heading for the aquarium gift shop. Shelly glanced at the front entrance that led up to the main exhibit, and she spotted the new security system and alarms installed on the doors. She'd overheard her father talking on the phone with the police, saying that somebody had been trying to break into the aquarium the past few weeks.

But then the entrance passed out of sight as Shelly and her friends headed into a dark and narrow corridor marked by portholes. Only shadowy light filtered through the round windows, and undersea creatures darted past the glass. This was Shelly's favorite part of the aquarium.

Kendall nudged her side. "Hey, who is *that*?" she asked, cocking her eyebrow.

Shelly followed her gaze to a boy about their age leading a group of tourists past them through the corridor. He had curly black hair paired with green eyes the color of ocean shallows. His smile lit up as he talked animatedly, pointing to jellyfish spinning and twirling in a graceful undersea dance. Their transparent bodies glowed with bioluminescence in the large porthole.

Shelly shrugged. "Oh, that's just Enrique."

"*Just* Enrique," Kendall said in mock horror. "Major swoon."

"*Total* swoon," Attina and Alana said in unison.

Shelly studied his face, trying to see what Kendall,

Attina, and Alana saw. But all she could see was a friendly boy who shared her fascination with marine life. Everyone at the aquarium was family, including Enrique. She couldn't think of him any other way.

"His older brother Miguel is a college kid," Shelly said. "Miguel studies marine biology and volunteers here for his fall internship. Sometimes Enrique tags along to help out. He's actually pretty silly. And kind of a . . . science nerd," she added, the last words slipping out.

"Science nerd, huh?" Kendall asked, pulling a grossed-out face. "Never mind."

Suddenly, something gelatinous swam up to the porthole behind Kendall's head. It moved like a gigantic spider, only quicker, cutting through the water and blocking out the light.

Attina squealed and dropped her cup.

Alana pointed to the porthole. "Kendall, watch out!"

Just then, a slimy tentacle shot toward the glass.

3
OCTOPUS QUEEN

"**G**et that slimy monster away!" Kendall yelled, leaping back from the porthole and squeezing her cup of iced latte as she did. The plastic top popped off, and coffee splashed all over her pink designer tank and yoga pants, staining them a milky brown. Attina and Alana both screamed again and cowered from the glass, which frightened Shelly more than the tentacle or the sea creature to whom it belonged.

"It's okay," Shelly said. "That's Queenie, our giant Pacific octopus. She's harmless—"

Another tentacle slapped the porthole, making the girls shriek again. But not Shelly. Then Queenie unleashed a thick cloud of black ink and darted into it, her huge body swallowed by the darkness she had unleashed in the tank. As fast as she had appeared, Queenie was gone.

Kendall aimed her manicured nail at the porthole. "*Harmless?* That *thing* attacked me!"

"Actually, she's probably more scared of *you*," Shelly said, defending Queenie as if she were an old friend. "Octopuses only release ink when they're afraid. It's how they escape—"

"Look what it *did* to me," Kendall interrupted, pointing to her stained clothes. "And news flash for you," she said, staring daggers at Shelly, "I could have been seriously injured."

Shelly bit her tongue. She failed to see how an iced coffee stain could have *seriously injured* anyone. She glanced back through the porthole, where ink still clouded the water, and wondered if Queenie was on to something about her new friends. She pushed the thought away.

Kendall rapped with her knuckles on the porthole, which, Shelly knew, was against aquarium policy. "You hear that, you big ugly monster?" Kendall called out to Queenie. "I'm going to file a complaint with the school. They should cancel this dumb field trip next year."

OCTOPUS QUEEN

Shelly felt her stomach churn. School field trips like this one were the bread and butter of their family business. They depended on them to keep the aquarium running smoothly and to put food in the tanks and on their table. This was the day all the local schools came to the aquarium. It was practically a city holiday. Shelly spotted Little River Middle School making their way past an exhibit across the room—and she saw Judy Weisberg's familiar silhouette framed by the tank.

Judy was surrounded by the other swimmers from the Little River team—*rival* swimmers.

Judy was tall for her age and stood out from her classmates. Her curly black hair was cropped short, better for tucking inside a swim cap. Her tanned face sported a constellation of freckles that dusted her cheeks. She must have been swimming outside all summer to prep for swim season, Shelly thought with a frown. Between the separation and move, Shelly had barely had a chance to dip her toes in the water, let alone train.

Judy's friends giggled and pointed at Shelly, who felt her cheeks burn once more. When Judy caught Shelly's eye, she sneered at her. The year before, Shelly had lost to

Judy in the fifty-meter freestyle at regionals. *Badly*. And Judy wasn't about to let Shelly forget it.

"This aquarium *stinks*," Kendall went on, oblivious to what had just happened between Shelly and Judy. Attina and Alana desperately dabbed at Kendall's clothes to soak up the coffee stain.

Shelly tore her gaze away from the Little River swimmers. She had to turn her attention back to Kendall. All it took was one formal complaint to ruin everything. And a formal complaint from Kendall *Terran* would be the worst. Her family practically ran Triton Bay. Her mother sat on the city council, and her dad was the head of the PTA. If Kendall followed through on her threat, the school could cancel the annual field trip, and other local schools might do the same.

Shelly had to find a way to fix this, for her family's sake. "Guess what," she said, forcing a smile. "The concession stand has a new coffee bar. My dad installed it to boost attendance."

Attina perked up. "Espressos?" she asked.

"Lattes?" Alana chimed in, eyes wide. "Mochas?"

"Yup, yup, and yup," Shelly said proudly. "Better yet,

they make a *killer* flavored latte this time of year. And it's a double shot." She grinned at each of her friends.

Now she had Kendall's undivided attention.

But then Kendall pulled a face. "Ugh, but my credit card maxed out."

Shelly dug in her pocket, feeling for the bills and loose change crammed in there. Technically, it wasn't her money; it belonged to Dawson, her six-year-old brother. He'd worked all summer to save it up, selling lemonade at a tiny stand, and before she'd left for school that morning, she'd promised to buy him a new goldfish on the way home to replace Mr. Bubbles. Now, as she counted the money, she realized that it wasn't enough to buy lattes for her friends *and* a new goldfish for Dawson. But a new goldfish wouldn't keep her friends happy.

Shelly forced a smile and fanned out Dawson's money. "Lattes on me," she said.

"Hashtag FTW," Alana said, pumping a fist.

"Hashtag caffeine fix," Attina chirped, nudging Shelly's shoulder.

"Shells saves the day," Kendall said, linking her arm with Shelly's and steering her toward the concession stand. "After that tour, I seriously might fall asleep. You're a lifesaver."

A short while later, Shelly and her friends claimed their flavored lattes from the counter, then headed to the sundeck for fresh air while their classmates continued raiding the gift shop. Shelly caught Normie shoving a whole cheeseburger into his mouth by the concession stand, which made her queasy. Worse yet, he made a kissy face at her, puckering up his lips like a fish.

"Shells, you've *got* to use two straws to drink," said Kendall. "It's way better."

Shelly usually skipped the lid and straw altogether, sipping straight from the cup—or, even better, brought her own reusable metal cup *and* reusable metal straw, which she cleaned with a long, exceptionally thin bristle brush. She took the two straws, still wrapped in paper, from Kendall.

"Thanks," Shelly said, trying to act cool, like she slurped from two straws at once all the time. Feeling a tinge of guilt, she peeled off the paper and crammed the straws through the plastic lid, which made a shrill screech. She could hear Mr. Aquino's nasal voice echoing in her head: *This little straw could kill an endangered animal like that turtle—or poison our precious oceans.*

But she pushed it away and sipped her drink. The iced coffee hit her mouth way faster due to the straws, and the sugary drink was bitter and acidic on her tongue, making her cough.

"Cute," Kendall said with a giggle while Attina and Alana were busy sipping, almost halfway done with their drinks. But then Kendall added, "Don't worry. You'll get used to it."

"Hashtag BFFs!" the twins chirped, raising their cups to toast Shelly.

"*New* BFFs." Kendall wrapped an arm around Shelly and pushed their cups together.

Shelly basked in Kendall's words. She finally had friends again. And better yet, they were the coolest girls in school. Shelly had never been popular, and she enjoyed being at the top of the school food chain, like an apex predator.

Kendall, Attina, and Alana drained their cups and tossed them into an inconspicuous eco-friendly bin. Shelly decided to hold on to her coffee after a few more tiny sips. There was no way she could chug it all. Finally, they emerged into the fresh air of the sundeck.

"Check it out! Isn't it cool out here?" Shelly said.

Although it wasn't even five o'clock, it had already grown dark. The sun was setting, painting brilliant pink hues onto the sky and ocean. Shelly surveyed the open-air tanks. The water in them sloshed over the thick barrier, mixing with the endless dark waters of the Pacific. It was a unique feature of their aquarium, and one that allowed them to keep larger animals, like beluga whales. Shelly saw one push through the surface and spray air out of its blowhole like a sigh of relief.

Kendall frowned at the ocean. "It's, like, totally creepy. What's even out there?"

"All kinds of cool creatures!" Shelly began. "I mean, if you're into that sort of stuff."

"Creepy, yucky fish?" Kendall said, arching an eyebrow. "Yeah, no."

Shelly turned away to gaze at the waves, trying not to cringe. A warm wind jostled her braids, and the briny air smelled like perfume to her. She couldn't let them know just how much she loved the ocean, or that the sundeck was her happy place.

Shelly spied Judy Weisberg and her friends across the deck, checking out the pod of dolphins with one of the aquarium workers, who tossed fish into the dolphins' open mouths.

"Check out Little River," said Kendall, pointing to them.

"Hey, did you hear the news about the swim meet tomorrow?" Attina whispered.

Alana clapped her hands. "Coach Greeley says we're getting new suits!"

"Yeah, so we can beat Little River in style." Attina giggled with her twin.

"*New* suits. *New* swim season," Kendall said. "But *one* thing won't change."

"What's that?" Shelly asked, quickly avoiding Judy's nasty gaze. She was excited for her first meet at her new school but even more excited to have another chance to beat Judy Weisberg. The swim team was no joke. They practiced a lot more often than the team at her old school.

After classes every day, they met up at a big indoor pool, where Coach Greeley gave them drills after warm-up laps. It was the reason she wasn't starting the Kids Care Conservation Club chapter. Well, one of the many reasons.

"Obvi, I'm still going to be number one," Kendall said with a grin.

"Oh. Right," Shelly said. Of course Kendall was the fastest swimmer. At her last school, which was much smaller, it had been Shelly. But they had practiced in an outdoor pool or swum in the ocean. The indoor pool wasn't the same. The chlorine smelled stronger inside. The water was too still. No breeze stirred it, and no currents pushed her toward the finish line. At indoor practice, her times had been off. Kendall had been out-lapping her in the drills, but Shelly was still determined to try harder. She was used to being a big fish in a little pond, but at her new school, she was a little fish in a big pond. Not to mention Judy Weisberg was still way out of her league.

"Definitely," Alana said. "Nobody can beat you at breaststroke, Kendall."

"Yeah, Kendall. You're totally the best swimmer at Triton Bay," Attina added.

"Exactly. And being the best swimmer also means being the most popular," Kendall said. "We have to beat Little River and win the Bayside Regional Trophy this year. My parents promised to throw us the biggest championship party if we win!"

If that was true, Shelly was nowhere close to being on the popular list.

While her friends continued chattering excitedly about the big swim meet the next day, Shelly nursed her iced latte and wandered to the catwalk that spanned the barrier dividing the aquarium's enclosed tanks from the open ocean when something in the water caught her eye. She clambered onto the raised platform a few feet over the sea, looking down at the blue-black waves churning below. She peered harder at the sloshing sea. Two eyes popped open in the dark water.

The eyes glowed with a strange yellow light.

What is that? Shelly leaned closer to get a better look, jamming her feet against the edge of the catwalk. It was narrow with no railing. Technically, she wasn't supposed to be up there, but she did it all the time, despite her father's warnings that it was a safety hazard. Shelly squinted. The eyes locked on to hers. They glowed brighter. She started and reeled back. She'd never seen anything like it before. She blinked hard. When she looked again, they were gone.

Maybe her eyes were playing tricks on her. After all, it was getting darker out, making it harder to see. She ran through her mental list of sea life, but none had eyes that *glowed*. Sure, some, like certain species of jellyfish, had bioluminescence—a chemical reaction that let them produce their own light—but they didn't have eyes like *those. Not glowing yellow eyes.* She looked down at the nearly drained iced latte in her hand. *Too much coffee,* she concluded.

Just then, something latched on to her arm.

Shelly jumped and wheeled around, almost losing her balance on the catwalk.

But it was just Kendall, who had grabbed Shelly to keep her from falling over.

"Whoa there, I thought you were a total goner," Kendall said, steadying her. "What were you thinking, leaning over like that? We don't want anything happening to you."

"Aww, thanks. I—I thought I saw something out there," Shelly said, struggling to catch her breath. Her heart hammered against her rib cage as she thought about the eyes in the water.

Attina and Alana wobbled over in two-inch wedges that threatened to slip on the catwalk.

"I mean, I don't blame you for wanting to live a little, Shell Bells, but there are other ways to feel a rush of excitement," said Kendall, clacking her nails against Shelly's coffee cup. She then aimed a manicured nail at the ocean, where waves pushed up against the barrier, misting the friend group with icy salt water. "Go ahead, chuck it out there," Kendall said.

"Wait . . . *what*?" Shelly said, caught off guard. She must have heard her friend wrong. Her eyes darted from the plastic cup, with its two straws, to the signs posted all over the sundeck.

NO LITTERING.

$500 FINE.

Kendall narrowed her eyes. "Go on—throw it out there. I dare you."

The twins giggled. "Do it! Do it!" they chanted.

But Shelly shook her head. "No, it's cool. I'll just recycle it inside." She knew the moment the word *recycle* left her mouth that it wasn't going to go over well with her new friends.

"Wait, you're going to carry that gross thing around?" Kendall said. "Like, what are you afraid of—getting busted? Can't you do whatever you want? Don't you, like, *own* this place?"

"Her folks totally own it," Attina confirmed with a perky nod.

"Yeah, it's *your* aquarium," Alana added. "Everyone knows it, Shelly."

"Nobody owns the ocean," Shelly said in a soft voice. She clutched the cup tighter in her fist. The flimsy plastic crinkled, poking painfully at her skin. "It belongs to everyone," she said.

Kendall rolled her eyes while the twins snickered. "Don't tell me you actually *care* about those stupid fish? Besides, it serves those disgusting creatures right. Just look at my new tank top." She stretched the fabric out, exaggerating the dark splatters on her expensive yoga clothes.

Shelly frowned, feeling protective again.

"Ha! I knew it!" Kendall said with a triumphant whoop. "You *do* care!"

"No, I don't," Shelly said, but her protest sounded weak even to her ears.

"Then prove it." Kendall's words rang out.

Attina and Alana watched Shelly with mischief in their eyes.

Shelly swallowed hard, tasting bitter coffee at the back of her throat. Her friends' eyes all looked her way. She held the plastic cup over the ocean. Several feet below, the waves swirled and frothed, beating up against the barrier between the aquarium's tanks and the untamed sea.

A million thoughts raced through her head. *It's just one little cup, right? What harm could it cause? Doesn't everyone litter sometimes, even accidentally?* Besides, she'd never do it again. *Just this once.* But still her fingers wouldn't release the cup. She thought of Queenie, and the leatherback sea turtle, and the dolphin pod, and all the sea creatures in their care, but then she pushed the thoughts away. She glanced at her friends, watching her with twinkling, eager eyes.

"Hurry up, fish lover," Kendall said, puckering her lips. "Chuck it out there already!"

When Shelly still didn't budge, Kendall sighed, turned, and headed down the catwalk. The twins wobbled after her. The moment was slipping by Shelly. Her heart raced.

Fit in at all costs. With that reminder, Shelly forced her fingers, one by one, to release the cup. It dropped from her hand, catching on the breeze and sailing to the sea. It landed on a wave, where it floated and bobbed. Shelly looked at her friends, who broke into hearty, genuine smiles.

"Nice job, Shells!" exclaimed Kendall, hugging her. "Knew you had it in you."

"Uh, thanks," said Shelly, giggling.

Attina and Alana also hugged Shelly, and the girls all whooped and cheered for her.

She'd done it. She'd achieved true friendship status.

"Maybe we can make this a tradition," said Kendall. "Visiting the aquarium the day before our first meet."

Shelly's stomach lurched, but she felt hopeful: this meant Kendall wouldn't send in a complaint after all and risk discontinuing class field trips to the aquarium. Shelly nodded at her.

"All right, let's head back," said Kendall, leading the twins across the catwalk.

But Shelly couldn't fight her guilt, and she glanced back out to sea. There, atop a white-capped wave, bobbed the cup before something reached up . . . and pulled it under. It looked like a black tentacle. Shelly blinked. But the cup was gone, along with whatever thing had grabbed it.

"Did you *see* that?" Shelly asked, but Kendall and the twins were already by the door.

"Let's jet," Kendall called back to her, "unless you want to stay out here with the fishes."

Before Shelly could follow, she heard a strange noise. It sounded like someone was laughing. And not in a nice way. Then the cackle was drowned out by another noise:

roaring water. The roaring grew louder. Shelly jerked her gaze back to the ocean, just in time to spot a huge wave that had materialized out of nowhere. It was ten feet tall and moving toward the catwalk.

Moving *fast.*

Shelly yelled as the wave hit her square in the face. It knocked her off the catwalk and sucked her toward the open ocean. Then it pulled her down into a swirl of fizzing bubbles and dark water that crashed into her nose, mouth, and ears.

She tried to swim for the surface, toward the dim light overhead, clawing through the cold water, but the undertow latched on to her like a vise. Still she struggled against the strong current, gulping salt water. Her lungs burned and screamed for air. She was going to drown.

Then she felt something curl around her ankle.

Something slimy. Cold.

It tightened its grip.

And pulled.

4
SHELL-FISH

"**S**helly, wake up!" cried a familiar voice.

The first thing Shelly noticed was that she was freezing. Shivering, teeth-clatteringly cold. The second was that it felt like she'd just swum five hundred meters. Every muscle ached. She coughed, bringing up a jet of salt water, then flipped over onto wet sand and cracked open her eyes.

A worried face peered down at her. *Enrique.* "Shelly, are you okay?" he asked with a shake of his head. His curls sprayed salt water, and his clothes were drenched and clung to him.

"Y-yes," Shelly choked out. Her voice sounded hoarse.

"I thought I lost you." Enrique's eyes flashed concern as he helped her to her feet.

Her ankle buckled as he propped her upright. *He's stronger than he looks,* she thought. She glanced down at her foot. Her pants were torn by her ankle, and a circular red welt marred her skin. *How did that happen?* she wondered. Her thoughts spun. "Wait . . . w-what?" she uttered. She took in her surroundings. Waves rolled in the dark, moonlit sea beyond the beach.

How did I get on the beach? she thought.

"What were you doing on the catwalk? Miguel doesn't let me go up there. It's not safe."

Shelly searched her foggy memory. *The catwalk . . . the plastic cup in the ocean . . .*

"You're lucky I was nearby," Enrique went on, wringing the bottom of his sopping shirt. "I was helping with the dolphins on the sundeck when I heard your friends scream. Well, more like *shriek.* And when I turned around, I saw a huge wave come out of nowhere and hit you."

That's right, Shelly thought. *The wave.*

"Don't worry, your friends are fine," he added with a lopsided grin. "Just a bit shaken."

Her memory snapped back into focus. The glowing eyes. The wave sweeping her off the catwalk. Shelly trying to swim back to the surface and being pulled down, then . . . nothing.

"Y-you saved me," Shelly stammered. "Thank you."

"Don't mention it," said Enrique. "Lucky I'm in training to be a lifeguard next summer."

"Right . . . really lucky," she said, in shock that she hadn't suffered a worse fate. "Thank you again. Hey, where are Mr. Aquino and the rest of the class? Are they still here?"

"No sweat," Enrique said. "Everyone's at the bus. Oh! I almost forgot!" He dug his hands into his jeans pocket. "When I pulled you out, you were holding this. You didn't want to let it go." He held out a nautilus shell. It was about the size of her fist and gleamed in the moonlight.

Shelly took it from Enrique. She ran her fingers over the nautilus's edges. The smooth enamel was yellowish, and it wound inward to a perfect pink spiral. "That's really weird," she said.

"What is?" he asked.

She bit her lip. "I—I don't remember picking it up," she said.

"You're okay!" Kendall wobbled up the beach with Attina and Alana.

Shelly quickly pocketed the nautilus.

"Did you see the size of that wave?" Attina added.

"Shelly, you're lucky you didn't drown!" said Alana.

"Yeah. It came out of nowhere," Shelly said, grateful that her friends cared.

"Enrique, like, *totally* saved you, Shells," said Kendall.

He nodded. "Sometimes big waves appear, caused by a big boat, or an underwater earthquake, or a volcano. Anyway, she's lucky I was nearby. It could have been much worse."

"See, girls? This is why we *only* swim in pools," Kendall said with a shudder. "Told you the ocean was dangerous. I'm telling my mom to cancel the aquarium field trip next year."

Shelly didn't have the energy to argue about it.

Everything that had happened hit her at once, and all she wanted was to lie down. Her shoulders sagged and her knees buckled.

Just then, Mr. Aquino ran up to them on the beach. His eyes fell on her and widened in concern. "Shelly, what happened to you? Why are you soaking wet?"

"I was on the sundeck . . . and a giant wave swept me out to sea," she said, her voice still raspy. "But Enrique saved me. He works here sometimes."

"This field trip is dangerous, like I said," Kendall snorted.

"Let's fetch your parents," Mr. Aquino said. "I'm sure they'll want to take you home."

Shelly's mind flashed to how swamped her mom and dad were at work, not to mention stressed over the finances. The last thing she wanted was to be another thing her parents had to worry about, especially when it was just a little water.

"No, I'm fine," Shelly protested. "I'd rather go back to school. I'm used to being in the water."

"All right then. Let's at least get you dry."

After thanking Enrique, Mr. Aquino helped her back

up the beach toward the aquarium. It was lit up against the dark sky like a sea palace. Shelly glanced back at the ocean. That was when she saw them: the two glowing yellow eyes—staring at her.

Then the eyes diverged, swimming in different directions until they were suddenly swallowed up by the dark waves. Shelly took the nautilus out of her pocket and clutched it in her hand, feeling chills.

The bus was already loaded with her classmates and ready to whisk her back to school, where her mother would pick her up after swim practice later. Shelly glanced through the window at Enrique. She could barely make out his silhouette in the dim light, but he lifted one hand to wave goodbye. *He saved me,* she thought. She didn't want to think about what would have happened if he hadn't.

For some reason, Kendall got out of her seat beside Shelly and moved to an empty row toward the front of the bus, and the twins followed her silently. Shelly didn't know why they were acting so weird, but she hoped it didn't have to do with her almost dying or Enrique.

Maybe littering wasn't worth it after all, she thought sourly.

But still she was determined to smooth things out with the girls the first chance she got. For now she needed a breather and was somewhat relieved to be alone at the back of the bus.

* * *

"Shell-fish, did you get it?" Dawson hounded Shelly the second she walked into the kitchen. Her mom went directly to her bedroom and shut the door.

"Go away," Shelly said, feeling exhaustion in every inch of her body. She glanced around the kitchen. Dirty dishes were stacked in the sink. Overflowing trash needed to be taken out. Dawson's algae-covered fish tank sat on the counter, needing to be cleaned for a new occupant.

"So, what kind of fish did you get?" Dawson asked.

She had to think of something—and *fast.* "Well, I didn't get you a goldfish, exactly," she said, knowing she had to play this just right to avoid a major Dawson meltdown that would result in her losing her phone privileges or getting grounded and having to skip the swim meet the next day.

"Another *kind* of fish?" Dawson asked. "I miss Mr. Bubbles so much. He was the best."

Now Shelly felt even worse. She loved animals of all kinds, but the truth was that Mr. Bubbles had been pretty dull. He never did much of anything. His most dramatic act was doing a lifeless bob and taking a ride down their plumbing. "Not a fish," she started. But his face fell, so she plowed forward. "Even *better*. It doesn't even need food. And you won't have to clean its tank."

He scrunched up his face. "What kind of pet doesn't need food? Or a clean tank?"

"*And* it won't die," she added.

He frowned. "Like a vampire fish?"

She shook her head. "No, not a vampire fish."

"Fine, I give up," said Dawson. "What kind of pet did you get me?"

"This kind." She pulled the nautilus from her pocket. It shone under the kitchen lights.

His eyes lit up. "Cool! A shell! I love it!" He grabbed it and clutched it to his chest.

42

SHELL-FISH

Shelly breathed a sigh of relief. She was safe. Now she needed to eat dinner, and then she had to figure out which outfit to wear the next day, but her mind was on the swim meet. Shelly made herself a turkey sandwich, hurried up to her room to eat it, and got ready for bed. She laid out her outfit on a trunk at the foot of her bed and flicked off the lights.

The second Shelly's head hit the pillow, she fell fast asleep. Her bedroom dissolved, and darkness stole her away. Everything that had happened that day—the aquarium field trip, the wave snatching her from the catwalk, her almost drowning, Enrique saving her—had worn her out.

But even her dream was tense. She was swimming in the school pool but was swimming in place as her competitors raced past her in a wave of water. Judy passed her, then Kendall.

She woke spluttering. "No, I need to win!" The words escaped her throat. She took a few deep, ragged breaths, then checked her digital clock, which showed it was ten. "Only a dream," she whispered. She began to close her eyes, lowering her head back onto her pillow.

Then she noticed the strange light. Pulsing. Yellow. *Eerie.*

It broke up the darkness with staccato flashes. It was coming from the room across the hall. *Dawson's room.* She blinked and sat up, wondering if she was seeing things, but it was still there. Still flashing. She pinched her cheek and winced. Nope. She was awake. The light was real.

Mesmerized, Shelly climbed from her bed. Her feet hit the carpet. Her blanket, which was soaked with sweat from her nightmare, slipped away from her body. She shuddered, as if a cold wind whipping off the ocean had hit her. The room smelled like salt and seaweed—most likely from the canals near the townhouse. Goose pimples pricked her skin, from the cold, but also from a sudden fear. The light continued to pulse, breaking the darkness. Silently, she followed it.

When she padded into the hallway, the pulsing light grew brighter. Her toes sank into the thick carpet her mother had installed when they moved into the town-house. It was a small way to make the new place feel more like home. Her mother's door was down the hall, cracked open. Shelly considered waking her up. But lately when Shelly tried to get her attention, her mother just seemed annoyed. Though Dawson's door was shut, the glow lit up the frame and keyhole.

Usually, she avoided the little barnacle's room like an outbreak of Ich, the parasitic disease that made fish grow slimy white spots. She hesitated at his door. She took a breath, held her nose with her fingers against the fishy stench, then pushed the door open.

In the pulsing light, her eyes scanned her brother's room. She took a step, then shrank back. Her bare toes had touched cold water. Puddles, leading to his twin bed, soaked the carpet.

"Dawson?" she whispered, trying to gauge if he was awake. No one answered.

She took in the small room. Old toys littered every surface. The contents of Dawson's closet spilled out onto the floor, revealing his half-hearted attempt to obey their mom's insistent orders to clean up his room—*or else*! Dawson lay asleep, his small body curled up in bed. His hair was mussed from tossing and turning, and drool clung to his chin.

PART OF YOUR NIGHTMARE

There, resting in the palm of his tiny hand, was the source of the pulsing light.

The nautilus.

Its pink-yellow spiral glowed brighter.

Intrigued, Shelly approached it, her feet squelching as they pressed into the drenched carpet, one step after the other. Reaching out her hand, Shelly could see the delicate flesh of her fingertips illuminated by its strange glow. As if in response to her presence, the shell flashed faster and grew so bright that she had to squint. She froze when she heard a voice.

"My dear, sweet child. Go ahead. Don't be afraid." The voice was rich, and kind, and as deep as the sea itself. A voice full of laughter, it seemed to emanate from *inside* the shell.

"H-hello?" Shelly whispered, unable to take her eyes from the vibrant nautilus.

"Go ahead, dear . . . take it. It was my gift for you. Go on. Take it. Take it!"

Shelly touched the nautilus.

And fell through the floor.

5
PART OF YOUR NIGHTMARE

Cold water enveloped Shelly as she plunged.

She spiraled down through what appeared to be tangles of kelp. What was happening to her? Where was she going? Finally, she somersaulted to a stop in a dim underwater cavern.

She began to swim, holding her breath, not sure where she was going but knowing she needed to find an exit, to find air. But seaweed snagged at her ankles, trapping her.

"Leave here . . . turn back!" came a tiny, pained voice as clear as day, even that far underwater.

Shelly looked down and saw *faces* on the seaweed. And with her heart racing and air running out, she realized it wasn't seaweed at all, but withered gray life-forms with sallow eyes and gaping, contorted mouths. They were nothing she had ever studied or seen in the aquarium. They couldn't be talking to her, though. She must have imagined it.

A current gripped her and sucked her down.

She tried to swim against it, but it was too strong. Her lungs ached, fit to burst.

Suddenly, an enormous crystal ball clamped around her, and her mouth opened in a silent scream. But then the water drained from the enclosure, and she was able to breathe, though she spluttered and spat and pounded her fists on the curved crystal.

"Help! Let me out!" she yelled. Everything looked distorted through the glass. She could barely make out the underwater cavern. Glass bottles lined the rough-hewn walls, and there were glowing anemones and the eyes of those . . . *things*. She gasped as something huge, bulbous, and black swam past her. *What was that?*

"Lose something, dear?" The same deep, rich voice she'd heard in Dawson's bedroom emanated from the shadowy corner of the cavern. "So coy!" A black tentacle shot out of the gloom and rapped on the glass. Shelly cowered, fear gripping her.

"Wh-what do you want?" she gasped.

Suddenly, the black tentacle reappeared, unfurling to show off an empty coffee cup.

Shelly felt her cheeks turn hot. She knew tossing that cup in the water had been a huge mistake. She knew it had been wrong. But she had done it anyway. "I'm s-sorry," she stammered. "I-I didn't mean to!"

"Use my ocean as your—oh, what do you *landlubbers* call it? Dump?"

Shelly's heart thumped fast.

Then the voice softened. "But don't be afraid, my child. I'm here to help poor unfortunate souls like yourself. Souls who have problems that need fixing. It's what I do!" The voice broke into a dark, churlish chuckle. Where was it coming from? Was there a creature with tentacles that could . . . talk?

"What happened to me? Where am I?" Shelly said, her voice echoing in the crystal ball. Peering down, she could faintly make out some sort of clawed, spiny pedestal that held it.

"You are a poor unfortunate soul," the voice replied. "That's why you're here, isn't it? My dear, you can trust Auntie Ursula." There was another flash of something swimming through the cavern.

Shelly shied away from the glass, sitting in the ball with her arms wrapped around her knees. *Was* she a poor unfortunate soul? All the things that had gone wrong in her life lately flashed through her head. Her parents splitting. Her father moving out. Her moving with Dawson and their mother into the townhouse and changing schools. The Semester of No Friends, as she'd come to think of it—those few months at the beginning of the year. And now that she had friends—Kendall, Attina, and Alana—all she could think of was losing them. And where *was* she? Dreaming? How had she gotten there? Her memory was fuzzy, but she recalled the nautilus in the dark.

"Ursula . . . can you let me out of here?" asked Shelly.

"In time," replied Ursula. "But first, what do you want even more than that?"

That caught Shelly off guard. She thought about it and said, "To be happy?"

"Is that it? Come on, now. I'm a very busy woman. Go ahead and make your wish."

"A wish? You can grant wishes?" asked Shelly. The words felt funny leaving her mouth. How was any of this strange dream possible, if it even was a dream?

"Of course I can, silly girl," said Ursula. "Now, what'll it be?"

"But who . . ." Shelly began, feeling a stab of fear. "But *what* are you?"

"Oh, a good question, my dear. Some call me the sea witch."

"You're a *witch*?" Shelly asked, straining to get a glimpse of her captor in the dark. Something shifted in the shadows. She caught sight of a flash of what looked like white hair and a ripple of more black tentacles. Shelly backed against the curved glass, but then the voice probed at her again.

"Some called me the protector of Triton Bay, but not in many moons."

"Well, are you a witch . . . or a protector?" asked Shelly.

"Would you believe that I'm both?" A deep chuckle—booming like thunder—emanated from the watery shadows. "Now, hurry up and make your wish. I really haven't got all day."

Shelly couldn't explain it, but she felt like the voice understood her.

"One wish?" Shelly said, then bit her lip. She closed her eyes. What did she want more than anything? To patch up her family? To be popular? To get certain people to notice her?

Nothing was worse than having no friends. She couldn't let that happen again.

There was one way she could be sure to get some popularity points. She needed to win her event against Judy Weisberg at the swim meet and advance to the championship meet. That way she could help her team win the trophy. That trophy mattered more than anything to Kendall, so Shelly had to do everything she could to help Kendall get her hands on it.

Shelly opened her eyes. "I want to be the fastest swimmer in Triton Bay," she said, "so we can win the swim meet against Little River."

"Oh, my dear, now, swimming is something I know a bit about." The dark shape darted past the crystal ball again. Suddenly, an image projected onto the curved glass like a movie.

Shelly saw herself in the championship swim meet. She dove off the block and plunged into the pool, easily outswimming her archnemesis from the rival school and winning the freestyle race. She swam faster and faster, slapping the wall far ahead of Judy Weisberg.

The image morphed into one of her standing on the top of the podium with a gold medal draped around her neck. Kendall and her friends, still in their swimsuits, swim caps, and towels, cheered for her with their coach. She saw her proud parents and Dawson rooting in the stands.

Her mother then did something wild. She turned to Shelly's father and hugged him. Was it possible they could get back together? Could their daughter's winning the race make them remember how great their family was? This wish could make everything in her life better!

It was so clear, just like the crystal ball.

The vision in the crystal faded, and Shelly found

herself staring at her warped reflection. "You can make all that happen?" Shelly asked. She wanted it so badly, more than she'd ever wanted anything. If she could be the fastest swimmer, then she could make her friends happy and, better yet, make her parents happy. Maybe even bring them back together again.

"Oh, my dear," Ursula said, "all that and more."

The vision reappeared in the glass.

Shelly ran her hand over the image of her family back together. She touched her friends' jubilant faces and the gold medal hanging around her neck. The scene began to fade away again.

"No, wait! Bring it back!" She hit the glass, trying desperately to make the beautiful scene return. But it kept dissolving, like a sandcastle washing away in water on the shore.

"Well, my dear, there's only one way to make it work," Ursula said as the image faded.

"I want it! Please help me!" Shelly begged.

"Don't fret, my child," Ursula said. "Of course I can help—provided you pay a price."

"Please. I'll do anything!" cried Shelly.

"Anything, you say? Well, I like the sound of that. I have something in mind."

Suddenly, a rolled-up piece of parchment materialized before Shelly inside the crystal ball. Hovering in the air in front of her, it glowed with the same eerie golden light as the nautilus had, and as it unrolled, a fountain pen with a bony fish tail materialized. Her eyes scanned the length of parchment as she read the ornate script.

"A . . . contract?" Shelly asked. She reread the words scrawled on the page:

I HEREBY GRANT UNTO URSULA, THE WITCH OF THE SEA, ONE FAVOR TO BE NAMED AT A LATER DATE, IN EXCHANGE FOR BECOMING THE FASTEST SWIMMER, FOR ALL ETERNITY.

"Go ahead and sign," Ursula said. "I don't have all day, you know."

Shelly swallowed hard and put the pen to the page, which rippled with golden light.

"Good girl!" Ursula egged her on.

Shelly hesitated, biting her lip. "What favor, exactly? What do you want from me?"

"Oh, my dearie, all will be revealed in time," Ursula said, sounding perturbed. She swam around, shifting in the shadows like a murky cloud of billowing smoke. Her eyes glinted hungrily for a second. "Great power was stolen from me by someone close to you. I cannot be a protector of the sea without it. All I want is for it to be returned to me . . . but all in good time."

"Great power? But what is it?" asked Shelly.

"Tsk, tsk. You're wasting our precious time!" Ursula's black tentacle emerged from the darkness and tapped on the crystal ball, pointing at the contract. "Do you want to be the fastest swimmer, or not? Many poor unfortunate souls would kill to be in your position right now."

Shelly studied the contract and considered her situation. Returning something that was stolen didn't sound so bad. Stealing was wrong, of course. If anything, it would be good to right an old injustice. But still something worried Shelly. Her mother always said not to act hastily.

"Can I think about it?" she inquired.

PART OF YOUR NIGHTMARE

"Think about it?" growled Ursula, no longer kind. "What's there to think about, my child? Either you want your wish or I've got better things to do with my time and I can set you free to swim back through my cave with the hope you get out before something comes after you. It's what a child like you deserves, for thinking it acceptable to throw your toxic trash into my domain."

"I'm sorry. Please, I just need a day," said Shelly, peering again at the contract. It flashed with an intense light, then vanished. Nearly complete darkness flooded back into the cavern.

"My dear, as you wish. You have twenty-four hours to return to my lair and sign the contract, or our deal shall be rendered null and void. No takebacks. No second chances."

Six black tentacles suctioned around the glass, cracking the crystal ball.

Seawater rushed back in, silencing Shelly's scream.

6

SOMETHING FISHY

Shelly woke, gasping for breath and clawing at her throat.

Gradually, the nightmare released its dark hold on her as she sat up. Her eyes adjusted to the dawn light streaming through her bedroom curtains. Her pillow was damp, and her pajamas were soaked. For a second, she feared that her dream had been real, that her bed was wet from being underwater. But then she realized that she was just feverish and *very* sweaty.

"Only a dream," she panted. "Only a nightmare . . . not real."

The piercing alarm on her phone erupted, making

her jump. It was intended to make sure she wasn't late for school, but mostly it just gave her a scare every single morning it went off. She jabbed at the phone in annoyance, silencing it, then lay back and tried to recall her dream before the details faded away. She remembered following a strange, pulsing light into Dawson's room. . . .

Why on earth had she dreamed about *that*?

But then more details surfaced. The nautilus . . . pulsing with yellow light. And when she had touched it, she was teleported into a dark underwater cavern . . . where Ursula offered to grant her a wish. *I want to be the fastest swimmer.* That had been her wish. She could remember it clearly. The details were fresh and sharp in her mind. *But it wasn't real,* she reminded herself.

With that reassurance, Shelly climbed out of bed, padded to her closet, and examined her appearance in the mirror. She didn't look feverish. She ran her fingers through her curly brown hair, still mussed from sleep. Nothing out of the ordinary, at least.

Shelly changed into her pink tracksuit and turned back toward her bed—and that was when she saw it. Her skin pricked. A soft gasp escaped her lips. "No. That's *impossible*," she blurted.

She rushed to her bedside table and blinked, thinking she must be seeing things. But no matter how many times she batted her eyes, it was still there, right beside her mermaid lamp.

The nautilus.

The one from the beach.

The one from her nightmare.

How had it ended up back in her room?

She studied it. Water had pooled around it. She struggled to understand how it got there. Dawson probably was snooping around her room again, like he always did. That was it! He probably left it there by mistake. How else could she explain it?

Feeling a surge of irritation—at both the nightmare and her snooping little brother—she reached for the shell. But then she hesitated. She didn't want to touch it. She remembered that touching it in the dream had transported her to an undersea lair. She didn't want to take any chances, even though she knew it was just a nightmare.

Quickly, Shelly used a sock to protect her hand while she tossed the shell to the bottom of her laundry hamper. *I'll deal with you later,* she thought as it vanished among dirty clothes.

With that, she flew from her room and to the kitchen. She quickly poured herself a bowl of cereal. A few minutes later, Dawson's voice rang out. "Mom, I can't find my shell!"

Shelly tried to ignore him and focus on her soggy cornflakes. But it was a lost cause.

A second later, her little brother charged into the kitchen with an indignant expression on his face. He wore a striped T-shirt, khaki shorts, and a red sheet tied over his shoulders like a cape. He had the same olive complexion and brown eyes as his sister, but his dark hair had an uneven, choppy bowl cut from when he had tried to give himself a new hairstyle, much to their mother's horror. Now he was banned from playing with the scissors. He put his hands on his hips and squared off to face her. "I bet Shelly stole it!" he added.

Shelly glared at him. "I didn't steal it. Besides, why would I give it to you just to take it?"

"Because it's *special*," Dawson said. "And you're Shell-fish!"

Shelly rolled her eyes. "You probably lost it in that dumpster you call a room."

Their mother ambled into the kitchen, workbag slung over her shoulder. "What's wrong?"

"Mom, Shelly stole my shell," Dawson whined. "And now she's lying about it!"

Shelly rolled her eyes. "Mom, I didn't steal it. He probably lost it."

"Liar pants!" he cried.

"Shelly, did you take it?" her mother asked. "Maybe on accident?"

Shelly felt sick. She shrugged, not sure what to say. *Had* she stolen it? Had she been sleepwalking and taken it? Had Dawson been snooping around and left it in her room? All she knew was that she couldn't afford to get in trouble. Not with the first swim meet coming up.

She had enough to worry about already.

Before she could respond, her mother checked her watch. "I'm going to be late for work," she sighed. "You two need to stop fighting all the time. Now please apologize."

"Okay, I'm sorry," Shelly said, feeling guilty. "I'll do better. I promise."

After their mother kissed them each goodbye and headed for the door, Shelly approached Dawson. "Hey, bud, it's time for school," she said gently. "Listen, I'll help you look for the shell tonight, okay? After I get home. And maybe we could clean up your room a little, too. Okay?"

Dawson snuffled but then relaxed. "Okay, thanks. I love you."

She ruffled his hair. "I love you, too. Now let's go!" After Shelly raced to the front door to grab her backpack, her eyes darted to her bedroom door, where a stain had formed on the carpet.

Wet footprints led from Dawson's room to her door.

Probably from him taking a shower and not drying off.

But it still sent a tingle up her spine. The nightmare flared in her mind.

You have twenty-four hours to return to my lair . . . No takebacks. No second chances.

The sea witch's voice echoed through her head. She shook it off, deciding to revisit everything soon. She didn't have time to worry about it all now or they'd be late for the bus.

* * *

The bell rang, and Shelly darted from the bus into Triton Bay Middle School.

She wove through the crowded hallway, hoping that no one would see her. She missed her private school, which was smaller and less chaotic. She headed straight for her locker, scanning the halls for Kendall and the twins in hopes of seeing her friends. They would cheer her up after her nightmarish morning. They knew that Dawson sometimes got on her nerves. But to her dismay, she didn't see them anywhere.

A few minutes later—though it felt like an eternity— she reached her locker. "Come on," she whispered, twisting the combination lock and tugging it, to no avail. Ever since she had gotten to middle school and had to change classes throughout the day, she had been having stress dreams in which she forgot her locker combination. She tried again. *Click.* It unlocked, and the metal door swung open.

PART OF YOUR NIGHTMARE

Right as a group of students walked past, rotten fish spilled out of her locker. They spewed onto the floor, their eyes wide and pale, along with a pile of plastic garbage— straws, plastic bags, old coffee cups, plastic bottles. It was the kind of trash that washed up on the beach.

The stench was overpowering, making Shelly gag. Worse yet, she stepped on a fish and lost her balance, hitting the floor with a thud and shouting out. The other kids turned to stare at the scene as more and more fish spilled out in a heap that coated Shelly's body on the floor.

She tried shoving them away, but they kept gushing out of her locker and all over her, their lifeless eyes staring. Now everyone in the hall had stopped to look.

Normie laughed. "Fish lover!" he whooped, nudging his friends.

"They're n-not mine!" Shelly stammered, pushing the slimy bodies off her and standing, holding on to the wall of lockers to keep from slipping back into the rotten fish pile.

Her mind struggled to come up with a rational explanation. Maybe her archnemesis, Judy Weisburg on the rival swim team, had planted them to intimidate her before the first meet? They'd face off that night in the hundred-meter freestyle. Judy was famous for pulling off elaborate pranks. Legendary, even. But then again, where would Judy have gotten all those fish? They looked exactly like the ones they fed to the dolphins at the aquarium. And also, how would she have snuck them into the school without being seen? More puzzling, how would she have gotten the combination to Shelly's locker?

"Fish lover!" kids chanted.

Shelly's face flushed. Now she was completely soaked in awful-smelling fish juice. She backed away from her locker. The fact that her family owned the aquarium made matters worse.

The other kids kept taunting her. "Fish lover! Shelly wants to marry a fish!"

"Tuna for lunch?" one kid quipped.

Shelly had never wanted so badly to disappear. Her cheeks felt as if they were turning into molten lava, like from an underwater volcano. She opened her mouth, then closed it, unsure of what to say.

"Look! She looks like a *fish out of water*!" someone cracked, followed by more laughter.

PART OF YOUR NIGHTMARE

That was when Kendall stepped into view with Attina and Alana, all dressed in their designer yoga pants and T-shirts. They stared at Shelly. Kendall shot her a worried look. Her dainty nose scrunched up in disgust at the stench.

But then Kendall set her hands on her hips and turned her ire on the other kids. "Hey, don't you *losers* have better things to do than make stupid jokes about fish?" she called out.

The twins joined her. "Yeah, hashtag *Losers*. Capital *L*," Alana said.

"Stop being lame and leave our friend alone," Attina added with a sneer.

Our friend, Shelly thought, warmth spreading through her body.

So they *were* friends.

The second bell rang, causing the crowd to scatter and rush off to their classes. Shelly slumped against her locker. Hot tears spilled from her eyes and dripped down her cheeks. This was turning out to be the worst day of her life—and it was only beginning.

But then Kendall wrapped her arm around Shelly. "Hey, don't worry about this mess," she said. "It's probably just Judy and her annoying pranks. But we'll show her tonight at the swim meet. We're winning that trophy this year. You're going to fly past her in your race."

"Thanks, Kendall," Shelly said, sniffling. "And you're so right."

"Hashtag winning," Attina chirped.

"Hashtag regional champions is more like it," said Alana.

"Yeah, we'll help you clean this up later," Kendall said. "I'm not the swim team captain for nothing! I'll get the whole team to help. You're not alone in this. We're on your side."

"Come on. Let's get you changed. I have an extra hoodie in my locker," Attina said.

"Thank you," Shelly said. As she followed her friends to class, she felt grateful for their support. But a sinking feeling also pooled in her gut. She couldn't let Judy beat her again. She couldn't afford to let Kendall down. Not after Kendall had just come to her rescue and defended her. She had to win her race at all costs. Winning meant she could keep her friends and prove her worth. And it meant getting revenge on Judy for her putrid prank. Her eyes drifted back to her locker, where the rotting fish and pile of trash still sat in the hallway, stinking it up.

Her nightmare flashed through her head again. The coffee cup she had dropped in the ocean. The sea witch. The contract and the offer to grant her wish. But she blinked to clear her head. The prank had nothing to do with her nightmare. It was Judy Weisberg messing with her.

I'll show her, Shelly thought. *And once I do, everything will be okay.*

7

IN A BIND

Shelly dove off the block into the pool as the buzzer sounded.

Her pulse thudded with adrenaline as she hit the cool water. Her arms tore through it with her feet kicking in rhythm. The straps of her new competition suit dug into her shoulders. Vaguely, she was aware of cheering echoing through the indoor arena. She could just make out Judy Weisberg's purple swim cap in the lane next to her. It bobbed into view every time she turned her head to breathe. Shelly counted her strokes in her head. *One, two.* Then *breathe.*

As Shelly's arms propelled her through the chlorinated water, everything that was on the line rushed

through her head—beating Judy, keeping her friends—
and she kept seeing the dead fish and trash spilling out of
her locker. Anger rose in her, making her swim harder.
She heard Kendall's voice in her head. *We're winning that
trophy this year. You're going to fly past her in your race.* She
had to win for Kendall and her teammates. She had to
win for her school. And most important, she had to win
for herself.

She couldn't let Judy get away with that prank. And
she couldn't disappoint her friends—not after they'd come
to her rescue when the other kids were taunting her in the
school hall.

One, two. Then *breathe.*

Shelly swam as fast as she could, slicing through the
water with her arms and legs in perfect rhythm. But after
the first flip turn, she started to lose speed. She still had
three more laps to go, but her arms were starting to feel
like molasses. Her legs were wearing out, too.

Maybe it was from almost drowning in the ocean the
day before? Terrible memories swirled through her head,
making it hard to focus. The nightmare. The nautilus.
The contract. Fighting with Dawson. The dead fish and

gross trash in her locker. Despite her efforts, she couldn't focus or keep pace with the others.

Especially Judy.

The purple swim cap kept getting farther and farther away, no matter how hard Shelly struggled in the pool. The water fought her every stroke, every breath, every lap.

Come on, you can do this! She turned her head to breathe but swallowed a mouthful of water instead, choking and almost losing her stroke altogether, which would disqualify her. This was *nothing* like swimming in the salty open ocean, where she felt at peace. This felt all wrong.

For three more miserable laps, Shelly struggled, trying to catch up with Judy but only falling farther behind. The purple swim cap was now half a pool length ahead. Shelly wasn't just losing to Judy Weisberg, though that was bad enough, especially since she still suspected that Judy had something to do with the dead fish. No. Shelly slapped the edge off the pool and popped her head up but didn't bother reading the scoreboard. She knew that Judy had won the race by a long shot. And like she'd feared, Shelly had come in last. *Dead* last.

Demoralized and exhausted, she hoisted herself out

of the pool. She was freezing and reeked of chlorine. One lane over, Judy celebrated her win with her Little River teammates. Their jubilant cheers only made Shelly feel worse.

Judy shot her an icy smile. "Better luck next time. Hopefully you won't stink like a fish."

The rival swimmers all laughed.

Heat crept into Shelly's cheeks. So it *had* been Judy who planted the dead fish.

Desperately, Shelly looked for her friends, hoping for moral support. Kendall, Attina, and Alana huddled on the bench with the rest of the team, with towels wrapped around them, wet hair, and swim cap lines on their foreheads. There was no jubilant cheering in the Triton Bay stands behind them. Just glum faces and glummer conversation. Shelly tentatively walked to the bench for a towel.

"This, like, majorly sucks," Kendall said. "I hate it when we lose."

"Yeah, it sucks worse than straws," Attina chimed in.

"Hashtag straws suck," Alana added, but no one laughed.

Shelly's friends looked crestfallen and deflated. She

felt terrible for letting them down. Like *next level* terrible. The kind of terrible that made her want to curl up into a ball and disappear. As team captain, Kendall took all their races personally, even when she wasn't the one diving off the starting block. While it was true that Shelly had swum as hard as she could—she'd tried her best—she hadn't swum well enough to win her race. Judy had sailed past her. Shelly realized that the locker prank had worked; it had gotten in her head. She had lost focus, had lost rhythm, and had fallen precious seconds behind. She caught Judy eyeing her with a triumphant expression on her face, but quickly looked away, feeling humiliated.

"I especially hate losing the whole swim meet," Kendall told her teammates. "Little River will never let us live this down."

Shelly wrapped a towel around herself. "What do you mean? We lost the whole *meet*?"

"Look at the scoreboard," Kendall said, pointing across the pool, to where the other side of the stands was beginning to empty out as people filed from the room.

Shelly studied the scoreboard and saw the final tally for Triton Bay versus Little River. Not only had Shelly lost her race, but coming in dead last had caused her entire team to lose the meet overall, despite Kendall's winning her fifty-meter breaststroke and Attina's and Alana's placing first and second in the hundred-meter backstroke. As if she could feel any worse.

"Next week is a new chance!" said Coach Greeley, their swim coach, in an effort to cheer them up. She peered at them through her thick glasses. Her dreadlocks pooled around her face. In front of her, she clutched her clipboard, on which she kept track of their times. "We'll hit the pool hard in practice this week. Everyone rest up."

Shelly followed the dejected team and their coach into the locker room. There, she and her teammates changed out of their competition suits. The new suits had looked so cheerful when they had put them on before the meet: deep navy striped with sunshine yellow, their school colors. But now they were sodden and balled up, and her teammates shot Shelly dark looks.

Shelly suddenly wanted more than anything to be alone in that instant. She glanced at Kendall, who had donned an expensive new athleisure outfit and was lacing her sneakers. The twins stood on either side of her, dressed and ready to go and glued to their cell phones.

"Hey, Kendall. I'm sorry I lost," Shelly said, zipping up her tracksuit jacket. "I'll work harder at practice this week, promise. I won't lose to Judy again. I can't believe she beat me."

Kendall frowned, but her expression softened. "Fine. Luckily, we have one more shot, like coach said. Triton Bay still has the chance to win the Bayside Regional Trophy this year."

"Yeah, it's only Kendall's life goal," Alana said, exchanging glances with her twin.

"Yup, hashtag winning," Attina said. "We've been planning it all summer. We're going to throw, like, the biggest party to celebrate if—I mean *when*—we win." She flashed a big smile.

"That's right," Kendall said. "My parents promised us. So don't ruin it, Shelly. Got it?"

They all stared at Shelly expectantly.

She forced a smile. "No problem. I'm just having an off day. I'll do better next time."

She would do whatever it took. She never wanted to feel this way again.

PART OF YOUR NIGHTMARE

Nothing was worse than letting her friends down.

"We'll meet you outside," Alana said.

Without another word, Kendall, Alana, and Attina took up their backpacks and left, along with the other swimmers. But Shelly stayed behind and sat alone on a bench as a million terrible thoughts circled through her head. She kept envisioning the next swim meet and Judy's purple swim cap, bobbing farther and farther out of reach. She had to find a way to swim *faster*. She had to find a way to beat Judy and win her race. She went to the sink and turned on the taps, splashing water on her face. But then something strange happened. The water tasted *salty*. Like seawater.

Not only that, but it smelled like the ocean when a breeze wafted off it and onto the shore. But that was impossible! The smell grew stronger. She even heard seagulls squawking.

Slowly, she backed away from the sink, still tasting salt on her tongue.

Suddenly, a familiar voice echoed through the locker room, even though it was deserted.

"*Ticktock, ticktock, my dear!*"

Shelly spun around. Her heart thudded. "Who . . . who said that?" she asked.

"*Twenty-four hours,*" Ursula said. "*That was our deal. Time's almost up.*"

But this is impossible, Shelly thought. *It was only a nightmare! It wasn't real!*

"*You may feel like a* fish out of water *now,*" Ursula said. The taps turned on their own, water gushing from them fast and flooding the sinks. "*But I can change that—I can help you win your next big race. Remember your wish?*"

The water sloshed onto the floor, pooling around Shelly's feet. She felt the urge to run, but something kept her rooted there. The sea witch in her nightmare had promised her one wish, hadn't she? Was it possible that it hadn't just been a dream? That it had really happened after all?

She remembered the contract, printed on parchment paper in ornate golden cursive, tempting her to sign it. Three words from the contract came to mind: *the fastest swimmer.*

Maybe it was a silly thought, but then again, hadn't her day been odd without explanation? Maybe this was her chance.

No more losing to Judy Weisberg and Little River. No more Kendall being disappointed in her. Better yet, if Shelly became the fastest swimmer on her team, she could actually help Kendall achieve her goal to win the Bayside Regional Trophy and throw the championship party.

This wish could fix *everything*.

"You . . . you can help me win my next race?" she stammered.

"Of course, my dear," Ursula said. *"You'd better visit me again before it's too late."*

"But . . . how do I find you?" Shelly asked, staring at her own reflection in the fogged mirror. She felt crazy for talking to a sink, with nobody else around. "How do I get back there?"

But the voice fell silent.

Then the sinks abruptly shut off. The water that had cascaded onto the floor ran down the drain. No smell of the ocean anymore. No more strange, disembodied voice talking to her.

But drawn in the condensation on the mirror was a simple swirl. It reminded her of something. . . .

The nautilus! Of course!

If Shelly touched the nautilus again, it would transport her back to the undersea lair.

Feeling excited, Shelly fixed her gaze on the swirl. That was the answer. That was the way to solve all her problems. She could keep her friends—and win her next race. She could pay Judy back for the embarrassing prank. They'd get the trophy and have the celebratory party!

Shelly took a deep breath. She knew what she had to do.

She just had to hurry—before her time ran out.

* * *

After dinner out with the swim team, Kendall's mom dropped Shelly off. As soon as she'd closed the door behind her, Shelly darted through the townhouse, zigzagging around the furniture, through the kitchen, down the hall, and into her room. She needed to get that shell and get back to Ursula's lair before her time to make her wish ran out. She dove for the hamper, which was shoved into the closet and stuffed with her dirty clothes, and started pawing through it, feeling for something hard. But her hands only sifted through soft, crumpled clothes. She dug deeper, reaching the bottom of the hamper. But *nothing*.

The nautilus wasn't there.

"Where is it?" she said in frustration, wheeling around. This was her one chance to fix everything in her life. She had to find that shell. Her eyes darted to the clock. Over an hour had elapsed since she was in the locker room. She searched her memory. She'd been upset from the nightmare—the nightmare that apparently wasn't a dream but was real after all. But she clearly recalled tossing the shell into her hamper before leaving for school.

Then she saw a note pinned to her mirror.

Scrawled in crayon was Dawson's terrible chicken scratch: I KNEW YOU STOLE IT, SHELL-FISH! YOU'RE NEVER GETTING IT BACK NOW!

"Dawson, where did you put it?" she yelled at the mirror, ripping off the note. Her cheeks felt hot with anger. Sure, she wasn't supposed to have the shell. Technically, it belonged to him. She had given it to him as a gift. But he wasn't allowed to enter her room without her permission.

IN A BIND

Dawson was many things, but he wasn't very creative. It had to be in his room.

She had to find it. She couldn't let Kendall and her friends down again. She needed the sea witch's help to win their next race. She flew through the hall and pushed open his door. Fortunately, Dawson was staying at their dad's house that night.

Piles of dirty clothes covered the floor. She couldn't even see the carpet underneath. Stray toys were strewn through them, just waiting for her to step on them and injure her foot. She started searching through the clothes, but there was no sign of the shell. She tried his closet, but it was so stuffed with toys it was impossible to make headway. The second she opened the door, they all spilled out. No way had he hidden it in the closet. There wasn't space.

She tried under the bed. On his desk. In the drawers. The bedside table.

Still *nothing*.

"Where are you?" she muttered, wiping sweat from her forehead. Her eyes darted to his clock and widened. It was almost ten o'clock. She didn't have much time to find it and return to Ursula's lair. Could Dawson have taken the shell with him to their dad's house? If he had, she was done for. Or what if . . . ?

Suddenly, a thought took the breath from her: if Dawson had found the shell, maybe it had transported him into the treacherous undersea lair.

Just as the panic of that possibility set in, her eyes darted to Dawson's bookshelf, where Mr. Bubbles's dirty aquarium now sat on the top shelf. She dashed over, reached up, and pulled it down—and sure enough, there it was. The nautilus sat at the bottom of the filthy tank.

"Thank goodness! There you are!" she said, fishing the shell out of the filmy water. But nothing happened at her touch. "You said it would bring me back!" she yelled, feeling silly. "Well, I found it! I'm ready to make my wish!" She clutched the shell tightly in her fist.

She tried yelling again and waving the shell in the air.

Fear rippled through her.

Was she too late?

No—she thought back to her dream. Shelly had asked for one more day—and the sea witch had agreed. It hadn't been a whole day yet. She had a few minutes left. She was sure of it.

"Come on, why aren't you working?" she muttered to the shell. Now she felt even sillier for standing in Dawson's room. Anyone who saw her would think she had completely lost it.

"Fine, I give up," she said dejectedly. "All I wanted was to be *the fastest swimmer* —"

As soon as the words left her mouth, the seashell started to pulse with its eerie yellow light.

Then, in a flash, she was plunging through the ocean, down, down, down. Water flooded her mouth, rushed down her throat, filled her lungs. She was choking, gasping for breath. Shelly felt like she was about to pass out, and then, suddenly, as if someone had flipped a switch, it was over and she could breathe again.

Shelly coughed and glanced around. She was trapped once more in the dry hollow of the crystal ball, which meant she was back in Ursula's lair. She could see that something large swam around in the shadows, just like before.

"I'm here. . . . I—came back!" she gasped to the darkness, pushing back against her fear, which made her want to scream. "I want to sign the contract. I want to be the fastest swimmer."

PART OF YOUR NIGHTMARE

A moment of silence. Just the shifting of shadows and the strange tentacles.

Ursula's voice echoed out. "Are you sure, my child? It's binding. There's no going back."

Shelly took a deep breath. "I'm sure. I want to be the fastest swimmer on my team," she said, trying to keep her voice steady. "I *need* to be the fastest swimmer. You promised to help."

Again it was quiet except for the soft hum of the ocean current swirling through the lair.

Then: "As you wish, my child."

Suddenly, the contract materialized in the crystal ball above her. In another flash, the fish-bone pen appeared in her hand. The pen shimmered with a golden light. The tip glowed with golden ink. She raised it over the contract.

I HEREBY GRANT UNTO URSULA, THE WITCH OF THE SEA, ONE FAVOR TO BE NAMED AT A LATER DATE, IN EXCHANGE FOR BECOMING THE FASTEST SWIMMER, FOR ALL ETERNITY.

IN A BIND

The current picked up, swirling through the underwater lair. Then she heard shrill voices rising from the water. She couldn't tell where they were coming from, which made them that much eerier.

"Don't do it!"
"...you'll regret it—"
"...can't trust her—"
"...she only takes!"

"I'm sorry, but I need this," Shelly said softly, more to herself than to the warning voices. She gripped the pen and pressed it to the parchment. "I don't have a choice."

She scrawled her name—*Shelly*—across the signature line.

The whole contract flashed with light. It rolled up into a scroll, then vanished in another flash and reappeared outside the crystal ball. A black tentacle reached up, encircled the parchment, and unrolled it, then scrawled a name onto the other signature line below Shelly's:

URSULA

"Oh, you'll be the *fastest* swimmer," she said, cackling. "You'll swim like a fish!"

Emerald light flashed through the lair, followed by a deep rumble of thunder. The ocean currents whipped up. The walls of the crystal ball dissolved, and once again the ocean claimed Shelly, choking her and expelling her from the underwater lair. As she felt the ocean sweep her away, a deep cackle made Shelly shiver with fear.

"Just remember our deal. After you win your race, you have to come back here. You owe me a favor. I gave you something, so now you have to give me something I want in return."

Shelly had a sinking feeling about what she had just done.

But she pushed it away.

I had to sign it, she reminded herself. *I didn't have a choice.*

She couldn't afford to lose her next race. Otherwise, she risked losing her friends and going back to that horrible new-kid-in-school purgatory, where she had to eat lunch *alone* and walk to class *alone* and do everything *alone.* Having no friends was the worst, the absolute worst.

Or was it?

8

GREEN AROUND THE GILLS

Shelly woke up clawing at her throat on her bedroom floor.

Her lungs pulled at the air, but something felt different. She couldn't explain it. It took longer to get enough oxygen. As she caught her breath and her vision cleared, she took in her room. Morning light flooded through her curtains. Half asleep and very groggy, she stood up on autopilot and staggered to her closet to pick something to wear. After she got dressed, she inspected the state of her hair in the mirror, wondering how long she'd have to spend taming it with the hair iron. As she gathered it up, she gasped and backed away.

"What is that?" she hissed at her reflection. She

stepped closer to the mirror to inspect what she had seen. On each side of her neck were parallel slits. When she breathed, the slits flared open, freaking her out even more. *What happened to my neck?*

She wondered if she'd injured it at the swim meet. But nothing jumped to mind.

The day before, her neck had been normal. She was sure. That wasn't something one failed to notice, like a zit on a chin that was just beginning to blossom. No, that was unmissable. They were completely noticeable, especially with the whole flaring-open-when-she-breathed thing.

"What happened to me?" she whispered to her reflection, studying her neck slits.

A door slammed down the hall, making her jump back from the mirror with a start. She was late. Any second, her mother would rap on her door and let her know that the bus was waiting. She had to hide her neck—and fast. She couldn't let her mother catch wind of what was going on.

What *was* going on?

Shelly rustled through her closet, her fingers coming upon a winter scarf from some long-forgotten family ski trip. It was far too warm for the mild California winter, but it was made from thick wool that promised maximum coverage. She started wrapping the scarf around her neck.

The door to her room swung open.

"Mom, she took it again!" *Dawson*. Her dad must have just dropped him off and he'd gone right for the shell, of course. His little face was blotchy and twisted up with anger.

"Get out!" Shelly yelled, shutting the door on him. Her eyes darted to the shell on her bedside table. She swiped it and stashed it inside her closet. She couldn't let him have it back; it had strange powers. Plus, she owed the sea witch a favor and she needed the shell to fulfill the deal.

But Dawson had blocked the door with his foot.

"You're not allowed in my room!" Shelly said. With one hand, she tried to cram the door shut while desperately attempting to finish wrapping the scarf around her neck with her other hand.

Luckily, Dawson was so focused on getting through the door that he didn't seem to notice Shelly's neck. At least, she hoped he didn't. Suddenly, the *click-clack* of her mother's high heels sounded. They hit the hall carpet and quieted, which meant her mother was coming closer.

"What now?" her mother said when she reached Shelly's room. "Open the door, please."

Reluctantly, Shelly stepped away from the door.

Dawson was pushing on it so hard that as soon as she released it, the door flew open. He staggered into her room and fell flat on his face. Her mother followed him in, surveying the room. When she saw Dawson pouting on the floor, she helped him up and looked hard at Shelly.

"What in the world is going on with you two?" her mother asked.

Before Shelly could answer, Dawson wailed, "Mom, she took my special shell again! I found it in her room yesterday, so I hid it in my aquarium tank. But it's gone again!"

Shelly felt a flood of guilt. He was right, of course. She did steal it back. But there was nothing she could do about it now. Carefully, she shut the door to the closet, where she'd stashed it.

Then she knelt down on the floor by Dawson. "Bud,

I'm sorry, but I think it's gone for good," she said, hoping he would leave it at that.

He sniffled and stopped wailing. "It's not fair."

"I'll get you a new fish for your aquarium. A real one! Like Mr. Bubbles."

"Will he have a black stripe, too?" he asked.

Mr. Bubbles had had a distinctive black stripe that marked his side. "Black stripe and all."

Her mother's frown transformed into a relieved smile as she leaned close to Shelly. "Thank you, Shell. I'm proud of you for working this out with your brother." Her mother glanced down at her watch. "Now, hurry up, you two, or you'll miss the bus and be late for school. And, Shelly, honey, please make sure your brother gets his homework from the kitchen table."

After her mother kissed the top of each of their heads, she looked at Shelly. "Why are you wearing a scarf?"

"It's the latest trend," Shelly lied, holding the scarf to her neck to make sure it didn't slip.

"Kids these days," said her mother with a laugh as she headed back down the hall.

Shelly snatched up her things, grabbed Dawson's

homework from the kitchen, and quickly tied his shoe-laces before locking up and heading out.

* * *

Shelly walked down the hall with her hand pressed to the scarf wrapped tightly around her neck.

Her eyes darted around nervously. She hoped nobody would notice how strange it was that she was wearing a winter scarf inside. Worse, this wasn't her only problem.

There was still the matter of the dead-fish juice in her locker. The day before, she'd picked them up and thrown them away to avoid making it smell any worse than it already did, but there was still the stinky residue to deal with. A few minutes later, she reached her locker—and stared up at it in horror. Something was spray-painted across the front in shoddy teal handwriting.

FISH LOVER

Who had done that to her locker? Was it Judy Weisberg and the Little River swimmers pulling yet another prank?

Or some other kid from her school who had witnessed the fish incident the day before?

She held her breath as she cranked in her combination, expecting the fish stench to assault her. But when the door swung open, her locker didn't smell fishy at all. The sudden disappearance of the smell was as strange as the appearance of the fish in the first place. How could the fish smell simply vanish? In fact, her books and smattering of pens were dry, without any stains or any indication that her locker had been filled with fish and slimy garbage. Once the shock wore off, she felt relieved. Why was she upset the fish smell was gone?

That was a good thing, wasn't it?

No dead-fish smell.

One less problem. Maybe the day would get better after all. Maybe she wasn't cursed.

A familiar voice echoed down the hall. "Don't worry, we cleaned up your locker," said Kendall, sashaying up to Shelly with Alana and Attina in her wake. "We all got to school early so we could surprise you." Her eyes darted to the fresh spray paint. "But we couldn't get that off."

"Don't worry," Alana added. "We reported it to the principal."

"Yup, she'll have it removed and repainted by this weekend," Attina said with a smile. "Your locker will be back to normal—and as good as new. Maybe even better than new."

"*You* cleaned my locker?" Shelly said, feeling gratitude for her friends. They still supported her even though she'd lost her race and cost them the swim meet.

"Of course, silly," Kendall said. "You needed our help." Her eyes darted to the spray paint. "Judy and Little River are so *lame*," she added.

"Yeah, hashtag lame," Alana said.

"You think *Judy* wrote this?" Shelly asked, nodding at the blue lettering.

"Like, of course," Kendall said, as if it were the most obvious thing in the world. "Who else would pull such a dumb prank? They probably did it to celebrate their win yesterday."

"Uh . . . right, of course," Shelly said, shifting her weight from one foot to the other and resting a hand on her scarf. She couldn't let them see her neck. She didn't need more problems.

"But you know what this means, right?" Kendall asked.

"Uh, what does it mean?" Shelly asked.

Kendall made a face. "Even more reason for payback next race!"

The twins giggled. "Hashtag payback," said Attina.

Kendall hooked her arm through Shelly's and pulled her down the hall toward class. "Don't worry, we've got your back," Kendall said with a wink. "We'll handle it for you. Oh, and odd choice with the scarf. But I don't hate it. Right, girls?"

Attina and Alana nodded.

As they walked into class, Shelly felt a ripple of happiness. Her friends had her back after all. They *did* care about her. They cared when she'd almost drowned. And they'd cared when she'd been pranked. They'd even cleaned up the mess for her. The swim meet and the fishy locker were just flukes. Plus her wish ensured that stuff like that would never happen again.

PART OF YOUR NIGHTMARE

Moments later, Mr. Aquino called the class to order. "Today we'll be talking about fish anatomy," he said, flipping off the lights and turning on the projector. An image of a goldfish appeared. "You probably learned a lot during our aquarium field trip," he added.

Snickers rang out in the classroom. Nobody liked science class except for Shelly. She tried to focus on the lesson, but her hand kept drifting up to check on the scarf. Suddenly, she felt a wad of wet paper hit her cheek. She jerked her head around. Normie made a kissy face.

Fish lover, he mouthed. His friends giggled from the back of the room. So they'd all seen Judy's latest prank. Shelly shrank down in her seat, feeling annoyed.

Mr. Aquino aimed his laser pointer at the goldfish's neck. "Class, what are these called?"

Shelly's mouth dropped open in shock. The little laser point hovered over the slits in the fish's neck. She knew *exactly* what they were called. But that wasn't why she was freaked out.

She reached under her scarf and touched her neck, feeling the slits.

When no one answered, Mr. Aquino shifted his gaze. "Shelly, care to enlighten us?"

But she couldn't say it. Her mouth felt dry, like it was filled with cotton balls. She quickly pulled her hand out from under the scarf. She suddenly remembered the sea witch's words, and somehow, it all fell into place: *Oh, you'll be the* fastest *swimmer. You'll swim like a fish!*

This was the gift from the sea witch. Ursula had given her *gills!* But that wasn't what Shelly had meant when she made her wish. She didn't mean for it to happen like this. Another spitball hit her cheek.

Fish lover, Normie mouthed at her.

The silence stretched.

Shelly started to feel like she couldn't breathe. Her chest felt tight. Her lungs screamed. Since the slits had appeared on her neck, breathing seemed harder. It wasn't her imagination, either. It had something to do with the gills. She was certain.

Mr. Aquino looked worried. "Shelly, is everything okay?"

But all she could think about was her neck, and

Normie, and the horrible nickname, and how if the other kids saw her, well, her new fishlike parts, it would only get worse.

Much, much worse.

"Uh . . . can I use the bathroom?" she managed to utter, then grabbed the hall pass and bolted from class. She had to figure out more about the gills—and how to make them go away before anyone could notice them. Shelly rushed into the bathroom, checking to make sure nobody was in there. Fortunately, it was empty. Slowly, she unwrapped the scarf from her neck, revealing the gills in all their fishy glory. She breathed deep, watching as they flared open, then sealed up.

It would be kind of cool—if they weren't *on* her *neck*. Like a crazy science experiment.

She was reaching up to touch the gills when she heard something.

The sound came from one of the stalls.

It sounded like something wet flopping around.

"H-hello?" she stammered, quickly rewrapping her neck. "Is anybody in here?"

Nobody answered. It sounded like the noise was

coming from the closest bathroom stall. The door was cracked open a bit. She approached it and then pushed it the rest of the way open. The strange noise was definitely coming from inside the toilet bowl.

She held her breath and peered into it.

Then she gasped.

A goldfish floated perfectly still inside the toilet bowl.

She couldn't be sure, but the fish looked an awful lot like Mr. Bubbles. So then . . . how was he here? She recognized the black stripe down its side. It was *definitely* Mr. Bubbles.

She leaned closer, trying to inspect the fish. On second thought, it probably wasn't Mr. Bubbles. A lot of goldfish looked alike. But then again, what was a goldfish doing in the toilet in the girls' bathroom? Was this another Judy Weisberg prank? Or other kids from class?

Shelly's mind whirled with paranoid thoughts.

Suddenly, the fish began to thrash around.

Then he did something that made Shelly jump back in fear.

"Help me! Your brother flushed me!" The shrill voice came from the fish.

Up close, she could see that he looked bloated and decaying.

His pale dead eyes stared back at her; his mouth puckered at the air.

Shelly slowly backed away. "No, that's impossible. Fish can't talk."

But the fish kept shrieking. "You're just like me now! You're going to go belly-up!"

Shelly slammed the toilet lid.

Fear made her breathing speed up and adrenaline rush through her veins.

But the fish kept shrieking. *You're going to go belly-up!*

Her eyes locked on the toilet, she backed out of the stall.

And bumped into somebody standing behind her.

9

THE FASTEST SWIMMER

Shelly whirled around and came face to face with . . .

Kendall?

"Hey, you've been gone awhile," Kendall said, clutching the other hall pass.

Shelly gulped for air. "Uh, really?" she stammered, feeling her heart racing.

Could Kendall hear the fish, too? Shelly's eyes darted back to the bathroom stall. She felt tense with fear. She strained to listen for the high-pitched voice that had emanated from under the lid.

"Yeah, Mr. Aquino sent me to find you," Kendall said, twirling her hair and studying her perfectly glossed lips in the grimy mirror. "Guess he was worried after you didn't totally nerd out on that fish anatomy question."

"What question?" Shelly said, distracted. She couldn't keep her eyes off the stall.

"Seriously, what's wrong with you?" Kendall said, spinning around to face her. "You look like you just saw a ghost. Is it Normie and his stupid nickname for you?"

"No. It's nothing. I'm fine." Suddenly, Shelly remembered her neck. She quickly checked the scarf, worried that in her panic it had slipped down and revealed her gills.

And she'd just been talking to a dead goldfish.

Kendall locked her eyes on her friend's neck, then they narrowed. "Seriously, though, what's with the scarf? It's cute, but it's like seventy degrees out."

Shelly felt her mouth go dry. "Oh, I was just . . . uh . . . feeling like I might be getting sick this morning. So my mom insisted I wear it." The lie tumbled from her mouth.

A tense moment passed. *Did Kendall buy it?*

Then Kendall snorted. "Moms have the worst fashion sense. You should've seen what mine bought me at Ever

After the other day. Now I insist on only shopping for myself."

Shelly forced herself to laugh, even though her mouth still felt dry and her heart was still pounding. The scarf around her neck felt itchy and hot. She was starting to sweat.

With another giggle and a shake of her head, Kendall headed for a bathroom stall.

The bathroom stall.

"No! Don't go in there!" Shelly jumped in front of Kendall to block her path.

Kendall glared at her friend. "Uh, why not?" she said, giving her a strange look. "I know the school bathroom is totally gross. But when you got to go, you got to go." And with that, she pushed past Shelly and opened the stall door.

Shelly cringed, waiting for Kendall to notice Mr. Bubbles.

But she heard nothing but the lock clicking, the lid opening, and Kendall taking a seat.

The dead fish was gone.

PART OF YOUR NIGHTMARE

How is that possible? How is any of this possible?
Shelly secured her scarf and bolted from the room.

* * *

"Wow, look at your time!" Coach Greeley said, clicking the stopwatch when Shelly slapped the side of the pool.

Shelly whipped up her head and snapped back her goggles. "How'd I do?" she asked, keeping her neck submerged underwater just in case. She didn't want anyone to notice the gills. This was the first time she had tried swimming breaststroke, but the coach had suggested it in case they needed her on the medley relay team. Breaststroke was Kendall's event, while freestyle was Shelly's specialty.

"It's not just a personal best." Coach Greeley scanned her clipboard through her thick oversize glasses, then looked back up excitedly. "Looks like it's a new school record!"

Shelly couldn't believe her ears. *"A new school record? Really? Are you serious?"* Suddenly, she was starting to appreciate the sea witch's gift. It wasn't a curse after all. But would she be disqualified for "cheating" if the gills came to light? Shelly would have to think on that.

After all, having gills *was* like cheating. The second she had dropped the towel from around her neck—where it was covering up the slits—and had dived into the pool for the practice drill, she had instantly felt something was different. It had felt like she *belonged* in the water. She had torn through the pool like a fish. The gills had worked wonders. She no longer needed to inhale on every stroke. Actually, she didn't need to at all, though she did once or twice so she wouldn't throw anybody off. *Just for show.* She didn't want anyone to grow suspicious about the girl who didn't have to breathe during laps. It was bad enough that Normie still called her *fish lover.*

"Well, it's not an official competition time," Coach Greeley went on, scribbling on her clipboard. "We can't add it to the record books. But you beat the previous record by a full thirty seconds. Let's see . . ." She scanned her clipboard. "That record was set last year by Kendall."

The name hit Shelly like a punch to the gut. "Wow, thirty seconds?" she asked. At the same time, she couldn't help feeling the grin spread across her face. Maybe the deal with the sea witch really was worth it, gills and all. She glanced around the pool. The other swimmers, including Kendall, were finishing the drill. Shelly climbed out and joined Coach Greeley.

Below, Kendall slapped the side of the pool. She was red-faced and breathing hard. She'd come in second, but a very *distant* second, in the drill. The twins appeared next, also winded.

Coach Greeley shook her head. "I can't explain it, Shelly," she said, studying her stopwatch like it was broken. "You're like a whole different swimmer today. What's your secret?"

Shelly, towel looped around her neck, shrugged and smiled, hoping that would be enough. But when she saw her friends watching, she said, "I guess practice makes perfect."

Coach Greeley grinned, then looked down. "Kendall, nice job," she said. "But you'll have to do better! Shelly here just beat your official record. Can you believe it?"

Kendall's eyes narrowed but then widened as she swept Shelly into a hug. "I totally underestimated you, Shells. You swam so fast!" she said. "Now we'll win that regional trophy for sure!"

Attina said, "You even beat Kendall at her own event. That's, like, *never* happened before."

Kendall flashed Attina a look but then quickly smiled. "Shelly's a natural at breaststroke," she said.

Shelly was thrilled by her performance but even more by Kendall's praise.

Now she couldn't wait to face Little River and Judy Weisberg again in the next meet.

I'll show Judy a thing or two.

* * *

"See? I told you I'd do better," Shelly said, proudly parading into the locker room with Kendall and the twins. She kept the towel draped around her neck like a featherless boa. She felt like her wish had been worth it. Now Kendall would just *have* to stay friends with her.

Kendall reached out and touched her shoulder. "As the team captain, I'm totally proud of you." Kendall grinned, and for the first time, Shelly felt like she had the upper hand in the friendship—like Kendall admired her, instead of the other way around.

Attina and Alana nodded their agreement.

"Thanks," Shelly said.

"Don't mention it." With a flip of her hair, Kendall marched to the showers. Alana followed, but Attina lingered behind, looking torn.

"Look, I shouldn't say anything," Attina said, eyes darting. She glanced after Kendall, making sure she disappeared into the showers. "But just be careful with Kendall. She wants you to win—just not *against* her."

Shelly frowned. "What do you mean?"

Attina waited for the showers to start running, masking their voices. "Kendall is the *top* swimmer at Triton Bay," she whispered. "Everyone knows that. She's the captain of the swim team. It's, like, her reputation. If you keep beating her top swim times, you'll ruin that."

"Ruin it?" Shelly asked.

"Yeah. Beating her that badly in the drill? At her own event? Surpassing her record time? Then parading in here like you're the captain of the swim team? And like you're better than her at the breaststroke now?"

Shelly felt her stomach drop. Her gills also flared, making her feel self-conscious. She clutched the towel tighter. "I didn't mean to do that. I was just trying to make her happy. And do what the coach wanted and was best for the team!"

Attina frowned. "Well, just know it's a sensitive subject, so be careful."

"I just want to win—to help us get the trophy. So Kendall can throw her party."

Attina shook her head. "Look, you're new, so I don't expect you to understand everything. But this is a big deal for Kendall. If you beat her in the next match, she won't forget it. Trust me on this one. I'm just saying this as your friend."

With that, Attina headed for the showers, leaving Shelly alone on the bench. She could feel the wet towel wrapped tightly around her neck—and, underneath it, the gills that flared every time she breathed. Wanting to race home and cry, she forced herself to head for the showers instead. Still in her bathing suit, she scooted into a shower stall and turned it on.

"What's good about being the best swimmer if being the best swimmer means that Kendall will hate me?" Shelly muttered to herself, stepping under the scalding water.

And aren't friends supposed to celebrate the successes of their friends? she thought.

She reached for the shampoo bottle. The water pelted her skin. She felt her gills flare. She had thought that becoming the fastest swimmer would help her *keep* her friends, not *lose* them. On top of that complication, she had actual gills. She'd signed her name in gold on that contract. She'd made her wish and agreed to the deal. But now she almost wished that she hadn't.

Was it too late to take it back?

Then she remembered Ursula saying, "There's no going back," and her heart stopped.

Mindlessly, she squirted shampoo into her palm—but thick oily black sludge came out of the bottle. It coated her palm and dripped down her arm.

She gasped, dropping the shampoo bottle. "What the—"

The sludge leaked from the bottle and stained the water black. It reminded her of an oil spill in the ocean. She looked down. Her hand was still stained with the oily black sludge. She tried scrubbing it under the scalding water, but the black stain wouldn't come off.

THE FASTEST SWIMMER

The sea witch's sultry voice echoed through her head. *"You can't change your mind!"*

A horrible cackling filled the showers. *"You wanted to be the fastest swimmer!"*

Shelly grabbed her towel and bolted from the shower, darting past Kendall and the twins, who were now dressed. She tried to hide her hand, hoping they wouldn't notice the black stain.

"What's wrong?" Kendall asked as she detangled her wet hair with a comb.

"Nothing!" Shelly said, her voice higher than she meant it to be. "I—I'm late for dinner!" Shelly quickly tugged on her outfit over her bathing suit and ran from the locker room.

The sea witch's cackling followed her out into the parking lot, where her mother's car waited for her. But as soon as she hopped in and slammed the door, the cackling ceased.

What is happening to me? Am I going mad?

And . . . what am I going to do?

10
SINKING FEELING

S helly hoped dinner would take her mind off everything.

Takeout containers littered the cafeteria table at the aquarium. Colorful murals of fish, sea turtles, dolphins, coral reefs, and other marine life covered the walls. The floor-to-ceiling windows looked out over Triton Bay, where the sun was dipping into the ocean. Soon darkness would fall. She, her brother, and her father had gone to the aquarium after school to order Chinese food.

But Shelly's father had been so busy with a leaking tank on the upper ocean deck that he'd forgotten to call in the order. So Shelly had taken matters into her own hands, locating the crumpled takeout menu and his credit card. By the time the food showed up, they were famished. Dawson was even starting to drum his fingers on the table. She had thrust the lo mein at him the second the food arrived, along with chopsticks, even though he ate with his hands.

"Sorry about dinner," her father said, digging into his chicken and veggies.

"No problem," Shelly said, reaching for the kung pao shrimp, her favorite dish of all time.

"Lo mein is like salty spaghetti," Dawson said, slurping up the noodles. "Isn't that cool?"

"It sure is," their father said.

Shelly cracked open the container she was holding and shoveled some shrimp into her mouth. But as soon as it hit her tongue, she almost gagged. She spat it out on her plate in disgust.

Her father shot her a strange look. "What is it, honey?"

Dawson cracked up. "Shelly's going to puke!"

Shelly set the kung pao shrimp aside, her stomach rumbling, and settled for plain rice instead. *What is wrong with me?* Usually she loved seafood. She had an uneasy feeling this had something to do with her wish, too.

116

SINKING FEELING

She wouldn't be surprised.

"Kiddos, it's really nice to have you here," their father said, looking up from his food. "Honestly, it gets kind of lonely during the week, even with all our fishy friends for company."

"Yeah, Dad, we miss you, too," she said, and she meant it.

She quickly wiped away a tear and finished her rice.

* * *

After dinner, while her father worked on the leaky tank and Dawson released his pent-up energy in the interactive play area, Shelly wandered through the labyrinth of the aquarium's corridors. It felt like a different world down there—wild, exciting, alien, and free. She loved being there more than anywhere in the world, but problems weighed heavily on her heart like an anchor.

She glanced down the halls, which were empty and dimly lit. It was after hours, but many of the staffers and trainers were still working, cleaning up after the busy day of visitors or tending to the many animals in their care. Usually, she'd love to check the pH of the tanks with her father or feed the dolphins their gleaming silver fish, but that night she wanted to be alone.

She pressed her face to the glass of Queenie's tank. "I wish you could talk to me. . . ."

The octopus seemed to understand. She swam up to the glass, her eight tentacles undulating in the eerie underwater lighting that filtered through the tank.

"You see, I have all these problems," she said to the tank, soothed by Queenie's graceful movements. "But I can't tell anyone about them . . . and it's the worst to feel alone—"

"Hey, Shelly, what's up?"

The voice made her jump, but then she relaxed.

It was only Enrique.

"Oh, hey," she said, playing it cool even though he'd caught her talking to an octopus.

"You know, I talk to them, too," he said, flashing a conspiratorial grin. He studied Queenie. "I think they understand us. Or maybe it's just my imagination. What do you think?"

How much could she tell him about what she knew?

SINKING FEELING

That there was deep magic in Triton Bay? That, indeed, some of the life down there could very likely understand them?

"Yeah, I think they do," she said.

"Right?" Enrique was staring at her woolen scarf. "Haven't seen you around much."

"Oh, I've been busy with the new swim season," she said, suddenly brightening. For a second, she forgot about her troubles. "I even set a new record time in practice."

"Wow, congrats!" he said with a genuine smile. "Glad you've improved since your plunge into the ocean. Just kidding, of course."

Their eyes met—and he held her gaze. She thought of how he'd saved her by pulling her out of the ocean. But then her hand returned to the scarf around her neck. She couldn't risk him, or anyone, finding out about her gills. She felt them flare. "Uh, right. Hey, I have to help my dad with the leaking tank." And with that, she ran off and left him standing by Queenie.

Why did she always act so awkward around him?

The truth was she liked him.

But somehow she always found a way to ruin it.

She always ended up acting, well, as Attina would say, hashtag lame.

What else could possibly go wrong?

* * *

After they had finished up at the aquarium and gone back to her father's apartment to watch an animated movie, Shelly tossed the half-full takeout containers into the fridge.

"Okay, time for bed," their father said, switching off the TV.

"You're the *coolest* dad in the whole universe," Dawson said with a toothy grin.

"And you're the *coolest* kid," their father said, mussing Dawson's hair. "Now brush your teeth. We've got a big day at the aquarium tomorrow."

"Just like old times," Shelly said from the kitchen. She'd always loved their family weekends at the aquarium. It was their little tradition.

Her father smiled. "Yup, just like old times."

Shelly started down the hallway. That was when she remembered she had to share a room with Dawson. He was a total mouth breather. After they had both brushed their teeth, changed into their pajamas, and wiggled into their twin beds, Shelly stared up at the ceiling.

"Isn't this cool?" Dawson whispered in the dark. "It's like we're having a slumber party!"

Shelly glanced in his general direction. "Uh, yeah. Totally." She resisted the urge to roll her eyes. She knew that all the recent change must have been hard on him.

"Want to tell scary stories?" he went on excitedly. "Rex told me a good one about sea monsters called sirens that sing beautiful songs to lure in sailors to eat them!"

"Usually, I'd love to hear your stories, but I'm exhausted," she replied. And it was true. She could barely keep her eyes open. It had been the longest day in a series of long days. She was looking forward to a cozy Saturday at the aquarium.

"Okay." His voice sounded sad. "I wish I had Mr. Bubbles. He always stayed up. Until . . ."

The day he went to the ocean in the sky, she thought,

finishing his sentence in her mind. Shelly felt even worse for being a lousy sister. She closed her eyes, wanting nothing more than sleep.

Drip . . . drip . . . drip . . .

Shelly woke with a start. She didn't know how long she'd been sleeping. If she had to guess, it was the middle of the night. She heard Dawson's snores. Was *that* what had woken her?

She listened in the darkness.

Drip . . . drip . . . drip . . . It wasn't loud, but it was driving her crazy.

She climbed from the bed and plodded out of the room and across the apartment on autopilot. Just as she had thought, the kitchen faucet was leaking. She tried to shut it off, but when she turned the knob, the faucet started dripping even more. And more. Puzzled, she tried twisting the knob the other way, but the water kept flowing. She flicked on the light and put her head near the opening to study the problem. Suddenly, murky black water gushed out of the faucet.

It didn't look like water. It looked more like . . . *squid ink.*

SINKING FEELING

Like the kind she'd poured onto her hands from the shampoo bottle in the locker room.

And it was filling the sink, nearly spilling over its brim.

Then seaweed tendrils shot out of the sink drain and wrapped around her neck. They tightened and started pulling her face toward the putrid black water.

Shelly struggled to get them off, prying the sinewy plant with her fingers. She wanted to scream, but she could barely get out a breath, and then her face was plunged into the sink. Under the contaminated water, garbage floated by. She tried to breathe, but plastic bags clogged her gills and made it impossible. Stars danced in her vision. A voice sounded in her ears.

You poor unfortunate soul! Don't forget our deal—or else!

She screamed under the black water.

11

WEBBED

Shelly's father flipped on all the kitchen lights.

"Hey, you okay? I heard you scream." He wore pajamas, and his hair was tousled from sleep.

Shelly looked at him in a panic, clawing at her neck, but nothing was wrapped around it. Fortunately, her father was still half asleep, and it was dark, so he couldn't see her gills. But that was the least of her troubles. She had almost drowned in the kitchen sink, which, now that she looked at it, was empty, no black ink or plastic garbage in sight.

"Uh, I—I think I was sleepwalking," she stammered. The lie slipped from her lips.

He screwed up his mouth. "Everything okay?"

"No. I mean, yes. I'm fine," she said, working to slow her breathing.

Her father grabbed a glass and filled it from the tap, and she watched, frozen in horror.

But only clean water filled the glass.

Shelly breathed out in relief as her father took a slow drink. Once the glass was empty, he grinned and held it up to the light.

"I don't know why everyone insists on buying expensive filters these days," he said. "Triton Bay tap water is crystal clear—and it tastes great."

Shelly smiled and rubbed her eyes. "Right. Yeah. Well, I'll just be heading back to bed."

* * *

Shelly didn't sleep a wink. All night, she listened for the steady *drip, drip, drip* of the kitchen faucet. She kept thinking about the seaweed wrapping around her, pulling her into the contaminated water. Finally, morning arrived. She threw back the covers and ran her hands through her hair, but something felt weird. Her hair was snagged between her fingers. She pulled them back to inspect them, and her stomach dropped. No. It couldn't be.

Her fingers were webbed.

Panicking, she glanced at her feet.

They were webbed, too.

Thin, translucent skin stretched between her fingers and toes, connecting them. Terrified, she waited for Dawson to get up and leave the room, then rustled through the hall closet until she found an old pair of her father's work gloves. Combined with the scarf, it was the best she could do to hide her new abnormalities. She knew she looked ridiculous, but fortunately her family wasn't the type to judge her various clothing phases.

Across the kitchen table, her father eyed the old work gloves paired with the wool scarf. "The new fashion trend, eh?" He chuckled. "Back in my grunge days, I wore my dad's work boots and flannel to school." He patted her on the back, making her worry that the scarf would slip down. "Glad my old gloves are good for something," he added with a wink.

* * *

PART OF YOUR NIGHTMARE

The aquarium—which usually cheered Shelly up—wasn't any better than her sleepless night.

Instead of chatting with the staff while they worked or feeding the dolphins or reef sharks or any of her favorite sea animals, she searched for somewhere to hide. The tunnels under the main exhibit seemed like a good choice. She entered the dark corridor. It was lit only by the eerie light that filtered through the water, casting strange shadows. Fish and other marine animals darted past the portholes. The taunt of *fish lover* echoed in her head. She tried to shake it.

"Maybe they're right," Shelly whispered to her reflection. "This is where I belong." She pressed her face to the glass, feeling alone and misunderstood. Every fish that swam past reminded her of what was happening. Her eyes fixed on the sunken pirate ship and the trident. The trident was corroded, covered in barnacles, but underneath she caught a shimmer of gold.

That trident was old and warped. How could it be *shimmering* like that?

She studied the forked spear.

It happened again.

Another flash of light. Another shimmer of gold.

Suddenly, a tentacle slapped the glass.

Shelly jumped back with a start.

But it was only Queenie again. At least this time Shelly knew she wasn't losing her mind. Queenie was real. The sea witch . . . well, she couldn't be real, but then how else could Shelly explain her webbed digits and the neck gills? She shuddered. The octopus floated by the porthole, almost as if she were saying hello. Her long tentacles undulated.

"Hey, Queenie," Shelly said. At this point, the octopus was practically becoming her best friend. "Do you know what's happening to me?"

The octopus seemed to shake her body as if answering no.

But Shelly knew it was only an optical illusion caused by the water.

"Yeah, me neither," Shelly whispered. "I didn't mean for this to happen . . . not like this."

Glancing around to make sure she was alone, she slowly peeled off her glove and studied her hand. Webbing stretched from each finger. When she touched it, it felt like her own skin. She pinched it and winced at the sting. She couldn't even bear to take off her sneakers to look at her toes. Tears pricked her eyes. Hiding in the dark by the fish, she sank down to her knees and wrapped her arms around herself. She didn't notice the figure watching her from the corridor.

He had heard everything she'd said. "Hey, Shelly, is everything okay?"

She looked up, startled. Her eyes fell on Enrique, who was leaning against the wall in the shadows, and she yanked the glove back on. She stood up and looked at him. Shame and fear mixed in her gut. Why did he keep surprising her like that? Didn't he have better things to do?

"How long have you been here?" she asked.

"Not long," he said. "But long enough to notice you seem a bit down."

Had he seen the webbing?

"Well, I'm okay. Just tired," she said. That wasn't a complete lie.

His eyebrows met in a look of concern. He wasn't convinced. She knew that she looked even more ridiculous with the gloves to hide her webbed fingers. She wanted to confide in him—to talk to somebody about her problems—but she couldn't risk it. No one could see her like this. Not that he hadn't seen her in a worse state. He had saved her from drowning in the ocean, after all. But still.

"I've gotta go," she said. And with that, she bolted down the hall, leaving Enrique alone.

12
CATCH OF THE DAY

Shelly draped a towel around her neck and tucked her hands under her arms.

Then she dashed from the locker room to the big swim meet. She couldn't let anyone see her fish anatomy. That was how she'd come to think of it. Kendall shot her a strange look but didn't say anything. Kendall had her game face on. This was their rematch against Little River. That meant one thing: Shelly was facing Judy Weisberg again in the fifty-meter freestyle. But for now, Shelly could relax. The first event was Kendall's—the breaststroke. Judy was swimming in the race as well, and Shelly was ready to root her heart out for Kendall. She was about to sit on the bench when Coach Greeley tapped her clipboard and said, "You're up, Shelly!" She pointed to the middle lane starting block.

Shelly's heart lurched. "But I don't swim the breast-stroke."

"After that record-breaking performance at practice you do!" Coach crowed.

Shelly's eyes darted to Kendall, who scowled like Shelly had never seen her scowl before.

"Um, okay," Shelly said, stepping up to the block. Now she had to swim fast enough to beat Judy but not so fast that she would upset Kendall.

Okay. She could do this. She just needed to pay close attention to where both Kendall and Judy were in the water at all times. Luckily, her lane was situated right between theirs.

Buoyed by her strategy, Shelly took a deep breath and glanced at Judy Weisberg.

Judy shot her a nasty look. "Good luck, fish lover. You're going to need it."

"Trust me," Shelly said, keeping her towel over her shoulders, "you won't beat me this time."

The buzzer sounded.

Shelly dropped the towel and dove headlong into the pool. She cut through the water faster than ever before, her gills opening and closing and filling her with all the breath she could ever need and more, her webbed hands and feet propelling her through the water at high speed.

In fact, she was going *too* fast.

She tried desperately to slow down, but she couldn't. No matter what she did, she kept swimming *faster* and *faster*. Her arms and legs seemed to have minds of their own. She started to panic, but there was nothing she could do except keep swimming.

Why couldn't she slow down? With horror, it dawned on her. She had made a wish to become *the fastest swimmer*. The sea witch had granted that exact wish. What Shelly hadn't realized was she couldn't reverse it. She couldn't swim slowly anymore. No matter what she did, she would always be the fastest swimmer. For all eternity. After her first flip turn, she was already several strokes ahead of Judy and the other swimmers. Then after the second turn, it was half the pool's length. She swam faster than any human ever, possibly. After she had lapped all the other racers in the pool, she slapped her hand onto the edge and stayed put.

So I can *stop swimming,* she thought with relief. She glanced up at the scoreboard, and her eyes widened in joy—and fear. It was a new record, but while she'd wanted to beat Judy and win the race, she hadn't wanted to win like this. She remembered Attina's warning. Kendall would be *upset* that Shelly beat her top score in a real race. While everyone in the stands was focused on the scoreboard, Shelly slipped out of her lane and back under her towel, feeling defeated. From the bench, she watched the other swimmers struggling to finish the last lap.

Coach Greeley ran over to her with clipboard and stopwatch in hand. "Great job, Shelly!" she exclaimed. "A new school record! And this time, it's official! Better yet, it's even faster than your practice time. Wow! Just wow!"

"Thanks," Shelly said sheepishly. While Coach Greeley scribbled more notes on her clipboard, Shelly glanced at her team. They were out of the pool and racing toward her, cheering for her along with the crowd in the stands, which was missing her parents.

But Kendall was not cheering.

Their eyes met as Kendall climbed out of the water—and she glared at Shelly something fierce. Alana and Attina looked glum. They both knew what had just happened. They knew that Shelly had taken the record from Kendall. And this time, like Coach said, it was official.

Coach Greeley patted Shelly hard on the back as she addressed the rest of the team. "Looks like we have a new top swimmer at Triton Bay!" She beamed at Shelly, who cringed in response.

Kendall looked downright furious. Her expression sent a cold wave through Shelly. The whole reason she had made her wish—the reason this all had been happening to her—was that she didn't want to lose her new friends. But the wish hadn't helped at all. In fact, it had made everything worse. Kendall hated her. And the twins would surely follow suit.

"Shelly, where are you going?" Coach Greeley called after her.

But Shelly had rushed to the locker room, tears pricking her eyes and blurring her vision. She tried to change quickly before the rest of her team came in. She needed to get her gloves on and fasten her scarf around her neck. She couldn't risk anyone seeing her without her disguise.

She pulled out the gloves and slid one on, but in her frazzled state, she dropped the other on the floor. She reached down to pick it up when someone stepped on it. Shelly looked up. Kendall was staring down at her. She studied Shelly's bare hand—complete with its webbed fingers.

Kendall's face contorted in disgust. "What's that? Did you *cheat* or something?"

Shelly yanked the glove from under Kendall's foot and slid it on. "No. Not at all!"

Kendall squinted at her. "You're acting awfully fishy. Also, how could you take over *my* event?"

"What? Why? Didn't you want me to win?" Shelly said, scared of her friend's reaction. "So that we could beat Little River? I did it. *We* did it! What does it matter who came first as long as we got the trophy?"

"Who cares about the trophy?" said Kendall. "You were just being a show-off. And nobody likes a show-off." Kendall eyed Shelly's now gloved hand. "Or a cheat." And with that, Kendall stormed out.

Shelly felt as if a jellyfish had stung her right in the heart.

* * *

Shelly hid in the showers until all the girls had gone, and then she stumbled back into the locker room. When she cracked open her locker and pulled out her backpack, she felt the shell lodged in there. *The nautilus shell that started this wild chain of events.* That shell and the sea witch were the reasons she was in this mess in the first place. Sure, things hadn't been perfect in her life before her wish. But they were better than this. *Fish lover* taunts reverberated in her head.

Her body was transforming into a fish. Would it ever go back to normal?

She pulled out the shell and stared at it, and then—almost on impulse—she tossed it into the trash can. She waited for something terrible to happen, but nothing did. She let out her breath. It felt like a weight had lifted off her shoulders. *Good riddance,* she thought. She headed back to the indoor pool. All she could think about was the look of disgust on Kendall's face. It hovered in her memory with every step she took. Shelly's mother was supposed to be in the school parking lot by then to pick her up. As Shelly passed the pool, it was dark and shadowy. The main lights had already been turned off. Only the pool lights glowed, casting eerie rippling shadows across the walls. She walked along the edge of the pool.

Suddenly, out of the corner of her eye, she saw a dark shadow dart under the water. It created a ripple that curled from one end of the pool to the other. Watching it, Shelly skidded to a halt, her heart thudding. "Hello . . . is anybody there?" she called out, squinting at the pool.

That was when she saw it again. There was *something* in the water.

She peered over the edge of the pool and down at the blue-green water.

Glowing eyes locked on to hers. She staggered backward and ran.

But a thick black tentacle shot out of the water and grabbed her ankle.

"No! Let me go!" she screamed, digging her nails into the tentacle to try to get free. But the tentacle pulled her closer to the edge of the pool, where the glowing eyes and dark shadow waited for her just under the water-line. Shelly staggered toward the water, closer and closer, trying her hardest to break free. A cackle reverberated through the arena. It was the sea witch.

"Stop!" Shelly screamed, fighting to pry the tentacle off her leg.

She was on the cement floor as it kept pulling her toward the pool, closer and closer. The eyes watched her, unblinking. Shelly was inches away from being yanked into the water.

"You forgot our deal!" Ursula cackled. *"You owe me a favor!"*

"But I take my wish back!" Shelly screamed as the tentacle tightened. "I didn't mean it!"

"No takebacks, my dear! Come to my lair—or else!"

Shelly struggled against the tentacle, punching the slimy flesh, and finally it released its grip and slithered back into the pool. Shelly ran as fast as she could. The sea witch couldn't follow her out of the water—could she? *I'm dreaming,* she thought. *It's the only explanation. It's not real.*

But when she reached the parking lot, she glanced down at her ankle. There were bright red welts where the tentacle's suction cups had grabbed her. She rubbed the skin carefully, wincing.

Shelly climbed into the back seat of her mother's minivan, numb with shock. Her ankle throbbed. Her best friends thought she was a total freak. And the worst part was Kendall was right. She *was* a freak. And a cheater. She didn't deserve the high score. And she certainly didn't deserve friends. As the car whipped along the ocean parkway, her gaze drifted to the open sea.

One thought filled her head: she had to figure out a way to make this stop, once and for all. She had a terrible feeling the sea witch wasn't going to let her forget about their deal that easily. She'd escaped this time—but next time she might not be so lucky.

13

POOR UNFORTUNATE SOUL

Shelly biked back to the pool later that evening in a panic. The sea witch's cackles echoed in her head.

You forgot our deal! You owe me a favor!

Shelly had to find a way to put an end to whatever the sea witch was playing at. She had to fulfill her part of the contract she had signed, or the witch wouldn't stop haunting her and ruining her life. It was the only solution. She had to find the nautilus she'd thrown away—and return to the sea witch's lair. She had to find out what Ursula wanted from her.

But she also couldn't trust the sea witch. The "gift" of becoming the fastest swimmer had turned out to be a terrible curse. Sure, she'd won the swim meet and beat Judy Weisberg, but she lost her friends, was still part fish, and had to hide her body. And it was only getting worse.

She biked faster. The sun was just beginning to set. A brisk wind made her shiver as she stowed her bike and clambered up to the pool arena by the school. But the door was locked. She should have expected it would be. It was after hours.

Shelly crept around the outside until she found the window that led to the girls' locker room. She reached up and pushed it open, then slithered through, landing in a crouch in the dark. She rushed over to the trash bin where she'd tossed the shell—but it was empty.

"I'm so stupid," Shelly muttered through her teeth. "But I can't give up!"

If the staff had emptied the bins, then the contents would be in the dumpster outside. She crawled back through the window, careful to shut it behind her, then circled around to the dumpster out back. As soon as she lifted the lid, she was hit by the stench. Pinching her nose, she rooted through the trash until she saw a soft glow coming from the back of the dumpster.

Could it be? She reached farther, almost slipping into the dumpster as she picked through the disgusting trash; then she felt the hard outline of the shell. As soon as her fingers touched it, she experienced the now familiar, but still terrifying, sensation of being sucked down into the ocean and into Ursula's lair. She pressed her palms against the glass of the crystal ball.

"Took long enough, didn't you?" cooed Ursula. The sea witch didn't sound happy.

In the dimly lit lair, Shelly could just make out her dark figure swimming around. She caught a glimpse of tentacles, then a glimmer of Ursula's wide evil smile.

"I want to take my wish back!" Shelly screamed at the shadows. "This isn't what I meant! I don't want to be the fastest swimmer anymore! I don't want the gills *or* webbed things!" She held the nautilus in her hand. Her *webbed* hand. She drew her arm back and then chucked the shell at the glass. It magically passed through the barrier and sailed into Ursula's lair. For a minute, nothing happened. Then it ricocheted back into the crystal ball—along with something else.

It was the crumpled coffee cup with the two straws.

The one she'd thrown into the ocean before everything went wrong.

Shelly stared at it, then picked it up and inspected it. What did that mean? What did it all mean? She'd thrown it into the ocean only for it to come back to her. Defeated, she sat down and sobbed, gripping the shell hard. "I wish I never signed it. I wish I could take it all back. . . ."

The second those words left her mouth, the lair started to churn angrily with a current.

A cackle echoed from the shadows. *"No takebacks, my dearie! You signed the contract!"*

The shadow of an enormous tentacled body floated just outside the crystal ball.

"But I didn't mean for it to happen this way," Shelly said, feeling her heart lurch. "Please, make it stop." She held up her hands to show off her fingers. "I'm turning into a *fish*!"

The sea witch cackled. "Well, how else did you expect to become *the fastest swimmer*?"

"Please, make it stop," Shelly begged. "I'll do anything you want. Just make it stop!"

"Anything, my dearie?"

"Yes, I swear. I'll do anything!"

"You poor unfortunate soul," Ursula said in a sympathetic voice. "What fine timing."

Shelly felt a stab of hope. "Just tell me what you want—I'll do it."

The sea witch snorted. "In that case, I want the trident from your family's aquarium."

Shelly frowned. "You mean the old trident? In the main exhibit? But that's just a phony hunk of junk to entertain the tourists. Why in the world would you want *that*?"

Ursula sighed. "So many questions for someone in your *precarious* situation," she said. "It sounds like you don't want to help me. . . ."

"No, that's not what I meant!" Shelly backtracked quickly. "I can do it. I just don't understand why you want it, or why you can't get it yourself. You have powers, after all. Why me? I'm . . . I'm no one."

"Oh, come now, dear. You're *just* the one. And besides, I can't get it myself," Ursula said in an exasperated voice. "You know all the security they have in that place. Fish talk."

"Well, what makes you think *I* can take it?" Shelly asked.

"You believe in Shelly, don't you, boys?" Ursula said.

At that, two sea eels—moray eels, if Shelly had to guess—swam past the crystal ball. Each had one glowing yellow eye—just like she'd seen in the ocean: the eyes that diverged and swam in different directions.

Shelly had a bad feeling. "But why do you want the trident so much?"

"That doesn't concern you. All you have to worry about is retrieving it from the exhibit. And then your world goes back to normal. No more gills. No more *webbed things*. Now, no more questions, my dearie. This is your only chance. Do it, or you'll turn into a fish . . . forever!"

Shelly panicked. "No, I'll do it! Just promise to reverse my wish, and I'll get it for you."

"My dear, you have forty-eight hours," the sea witch said in her deep voice. "Otherwise, it will be too late to reverse your wish. And it will become permanent. Do you understand?"

Shelly felt torn and deeply unsettled, but she didn't

have a choice. She couldn't turn into a fish! She had to do exactly what the sea witch wanted. "Yes, I understand," she said. "I'll do it. I'll get the trident and bring it here."

A deep cackle emanated from the darkness. "Don't fail me—or else!"

Slowly, the lair dissolved into nothingness and the sea witch along with it. Last, the two glowing eyes of the eels vanished into the watery shadows.

14

SINK OR SWIM

"**W**hat's so important about this trident?" Shelly asked herself.

She stared through the thick glass while tourists milled around, oohing and aahing at the main exhibit. The reef shark darted past the glass, drawing excited squeals from the crowd.

But Shelly didn't flinch. The shark was harmless; he just *looked* scary.

But also, she had bigger fish to fry.

She kept her eyes fixed on the trident in the main exhibit, trying to process everything she'd just learned from the sea witch. The prongs pointed upward. The trident itself was badly corroded and covered in barnacles.

Behind it, a treasure chest overflowed with faux precious gems and ancient gold coins. Or at least, she *thought* they were faux. But then she remembered the other day. The old trident had flashed with golden light. She'd thought it was a trick of the eye—shifting sunlight filtered through water—but what if it was something else?

A sunken pirate ship towered over the scene while fish, sharks, and the leatherback sea turtle swam around the exhibit. Sunlight rippled over everything. The trident really did look like a rusty hunk of junk. But she caught a flash of gold again as the sunlight shifted, the same shimmering she had noticed the other day. It wasn't just her eyes playing tricks on her.

Maybe it was full of magic. And if it was, what did the sea witch plan to do with it? What exactly would she use it for? And how had Shelly's family gotten involved in the first place?

Enrique appeared behind her, clutching a slop bucket of fish to feed the dolphins. It was after school, when he came to the aquarium to help out his brother, who still interned there.

When he saw her, he frowned. "What happened to you? Looks like you've seen a ghost."

Shelly bit her lip. She couldn't tell him, *could* she? He'd just think she was imagining things. Maybe he'd even tease her about it. She started to turn away, but he stopped her.

"Come on, spit it out already," he said, flashing her a mischievous grin. "I promise, I'm good at keeping secrets. The dolphins tell me *all* their gossip. And my lips are sealed."

"The dolphins gossip?" Despite her stress, she cracked a smile.

"Yup, they're worse than my dad's book club." He grinned but then turned more serious. "Look, I see you here all the time. And lately, you've been acting . . . *different*."

"Different?" she said with a start, nervous he was on to her. "How so?"

"Jumpy. Quiet. Running away from me." He frowned. "You never used to be afraid before. It's what I liked most about you. But now, it's like something changed. Ever since I pulled you out of the ocean that day you almost drowned."

She hesitated. He was right—it had all started when she intentionally dropped that stupid coffee cup into the ocean and the wave swept her out to sea. Enrique had saved her life. Shouldn't she trust him? But something stopped her. She remembered Kendall's disgusted face in the locker room when she saw Shelly's webbed hand. "Why do you care so much?" she asked, torn. "It's not your problem."

He grinned. "Science nerds have to stick together, right?"

"Then prove it. What's the name of that fish?" She pointed to a bright orange-and-white fish floating in a sea anemone's glowing blue tentacles. Its adorable little face poked out.

"Clown fish . . . also known as anemonefish."

"Okay. And what are its attributes?" pressed Shelly.

Enrique studied the fish as the sea anemone's tentacles caressed it. "Well, it's called anemonefish because it's symbiotic with that sea anemone. The anemone's tentacles are poisonous—but not to the clown fish. Those tentacles protect it from unwanted predators."

"And that?" Shelly pointed to two eyes in the sand.

He rolled his eyes. "A flounder, obviously. Ask me a hard one next time, okay?"

Shelly giggled. He really was a science nerd like her. For a moment, her troubles dissolved, but then they rushed back in, like a riptide. She glanced around and lowered her voice.

"All right, something did happen . . ." she started, feeling completely paranoid. Tourists milled around the exhibits. "But you have to promise me that you won't think I'm crazy."

"I swear," he said. "Cross my heart."

"And we can't talk here," she added. "We need to talk somewhere private."

He lifted the slop bucket. "I know just the place."

* * *

Shelly and Enrique stepped out onto the sundeck, where the aquarium looked out on the open sea. The waves rolled uneasily in the distance while clouds built overhead. It looked like a storm was coming in over the Pacific. Cold wind whipped off the water and tousled their hair, bringing with it the briny tang of the sea. It was a smell Shelly had once loved, but now it reminded her of evil.

But instead of staying outside with the tourists, Enrique pulled her backstage behind the dolphin exhibit, where only the dolphin trainers were permitted. PRIVATE: KEEP OUT signs were posted, but Enrique ignored them. He was practically staff at this point. He'd been going there with his brother, Miguel, for a long time, helping out and learning everything—and apparently studying Shelly like some curious creature while he was at it.

Enrique tossed some fish to the dolphins, who gathered in excitement. He patted Lil' Mermy on the head when he swam up to the side. "Good boy," he said as the dolphin squeaked and snatched another fish out of the air.

"He is," Shelly said, forgetting her worries for a moment. The dolphins had that effect on her. And as much as she hated to admit it, so did Enrique. She could still remember when Lil' Mermy was born that spring in the aquarium. It was a big deal to have a newborn in captivity. The tiny dolphin baby had grown up and was basically a mischievous teenager now. Well, the dolphin equivalent, anyway.

"Remember when he stole my brother's hat?" Enrique said, tossing another fish.

Shelly giggled. "Oh, I heard about that. He snatched it right off his head, then dragged it through the exhibit to show off his new find."

Enrique smiled. "Yeah, my brother wasn't thrilled about that. He still had the original stickers on it."

"Hazards of working at an aquarium," she said, smiling at the dolphin pod happily munching on their fish snacks. "You know, sometimes I think they're smarter than us. And they're definitely more sensitive," she said, patting Lil' Mermy. "Just look in their eyes."

The dolphin purred and squeaked in appreciation.

Enrique looked at her. Their eyes met. "That's so weird," he said with a lopsided grin. "Thought I was the only one who believed that."

"Ha, same," she said with a smile.

When Enrique finished feeding them, Shelly led him over to the catwalk that crossed above the tanks, where they sat with their feet dangling over the dolphin exhibit. She looked down at the gloves hiding her webbed fingers. The scarf remained wrapped firmly around her neck.

He nudged her shoulder. "Hey, really, it can't be that bad."

She sighed. "You have no idea."

"Try me," he said, nudging her again. "Promise I won't judge. Is it about your parents?"

She shook her head. "You'll just call me nerd or fish lover, like everyone else."

"Well, I like nerds. Especially ones who are into marine biology."

Shelly hesitated. Kendall's sneering face in the locker room flashed through her head.

But then she looked at Enrique—his kind eyes, the prominent dimples in his cheeks. He wasn't like the other kids. Neither of them was. It was refreshing. She felt like he might understand. It seemed worth it to take a chance. Besides, carrying this secret around was making her even more anxious. What made problems unbearable, she decided, was dealing with them alone. That made everything a million times worse. She took a deep breath, feeling her gills flare.

Her stomach churned with fear, but she forced the words out anyway. "Okay then," she said, fiddling with her scarf. "I did see something, but it wasn't a ghost."

"Not a ghost?" he asked. "Well, that's good."

"No, it was a witch," she said. "And not just any witch. It was a sea witch."

She waited for him to laugh, call her crazy, or taunt her with names.

But he didn't. His eyes met hers. "Wow, a real sea witch? Did she grant you a wish?"

Shelly's eyes nearly bugged out of her head. "Wait, how do you know about that?"

"Don't tell me you haven't heard the old fairy tales," he said.

"Fairy tales?" she asked.

"Listen, my family goes back a long way in Triton Bay. My grandfather used to tell us all sorts of colorful stories before bedtime when we were kids. He was a fisherman," Enrique said.

"And some had to do with a sea witch?" Shelly guessed.

He nodded. "Yeah, but I didn't realize she was real."

"Oh, she's real, all right," Shelly said with a shudder. "And she did grant me a wish. It sounds stupid, but I wanted to become the fastest swimmer." Reflexively, she glanced at the ocean in the distance. It churned with blue-black waves. Was Ursula listening in?

"That day you fell in the ocean . . . is that when it happened?" he asked.

She nodded, took a deep breath to still her nerves, then pulled off her scarf, revealing her gills in all their glory. She expected him to recoil in disgust like Kendall had when she'd seen her hand.

Instead, he studied her neck in fascination. His eyes roved over the slits, and he watched as they flared open when she breathed. He didn't say anything for a long moment. She began to regret showing him.

Finally, he spoke up. "I knew you were looking a little green around the gills, but . . ." Shelly rolled her eyes. His voice trailed off, but then his eyes lit up. "Are those what I think they are?"

"Yup," Shelly said.

"Do they . . . work?" he asked.

"Uh, yeah," she said, feeling self-conscious. "I can breathe underwater. I found out at swim practice. I still raise my head like everyone else. But I don't really have to anymore."

"This is amazing! You have an actual superpower. That's so rad!"

"Yeah, I guess I didn't think of it that way. And that's not all." Shelly pulled off her gloves, then slipped off her shoes and socks. She splayed out her fingers and toes, showing him the delicate webbing that stretched between her digits.

His eyes widened. "Wow, you weren't kidding." Then he grinned and did something unexpected: he ran to the catwalk and dove into the ocean, letting out a joyous yelp as he plunged below the surface.

Remembering how the wave swept her out to sea the last time she'd been out there, Shelly ran to the catwalk and peered into the frothy waves. There was no sign of Enrique. Her heart hammered. What if he never came up? But then he suddenly broke through the surface.

"I love nature!" He plunged back under the water

and popped up again. "Come on, fish girl!" he called out, splashing water toward her. "Let's see what you can do!"

Shelly hesitated. The last time she fell off the catwalk, she'd almost drowned. But that had been due to a big wave. An unnatural one, she realized now. And back then, she didn't have special superpowers, as Enrique called them. She dove into the water, feeling the brisk crack of the surface breaking around her, then the reassuring touch of seawater on her skin and in her gills. Nothing felt better—or more natural—to her. She swam down deep, then aimed for the surface. She broke through it, almost like a dolphin, leaping out of the water, then diving back down. A wild pod of dolphins swam by and joined her in her underwater revelry, swimming around her and nudging her on. Enrique watched in awe.

She stayed under for a long time, then surprised him by surfacing behind him. "Boo!"

He startled, then grinned. "Watching you swim like that—well, it's incredible."

"So you're not freaked out?" she said. "You don't think that I'm totally disgusting?"

"Okay, to be honest," he said, bobbing in the water

beside her, "I am a *little* freaked out. It's not like you meet a half-fish, half-human every day, right? But disgusted? Not at all!"

"Really?" she said.

He nodded. "This is the coolest thing I've ever seen."

"Ugh, more like a horrible nightmare," she snorted.

"Nightmare? You can breathe underwater. And probably swim faster, too."

"Yup, I crushed the other swimmers at the last swim meet and broke the official record."

"No joke?"

She nodded, remembering her victory and feeling excited about it for the first time.

"When I dove into the pool, it felt like I belonged there. It was the most incredible feeling in the world. . . ." Her voice trailed off.

"I'm guessing there's a catch?"

"It's a long story," she said. "Basically, if I don't help the sea witch steal the trident from the main exhibit, then this will all become permanent. I'll turn into a fish *for all eternity*."

He blinked at her, taking that in. "Wait . . . the

trident? Why would she want that old thing? You'd better tell me the whole story. Start from the beginning. Don't leave anything out."

They waded out of the ocean, onto the beach, and walked back toward the aquarium, and Shelly told him everything from the beginning: Dropping the cup in the ocean. The nautilus and the nightmare. Making her wish and signing the contract, then waking up with gills. When she finished, he studied her.

"Wow, that is some story."

"You don't believe me," she said.

"Oh no, I believe you," he said, pointing to her gills. "Anyway, that's too crazy to make up. Plus, like I said, I've heard of the sea witch. I just didn't realize the stories were real."

"Wait, that's it!" Shelly said excitedly. "Maybe the old stories can help us."

"Right, there's an old myth about her. My grandfather used to talk about it. Something about her haunting sailors who got lost in storms . . ."

"Anything else?" she said.

Maybe he knew about a way to help Shelly that didn't involve the trident at all.

He shook his head. "It was a long time ago. I'm sorry. I don't remember very much."

"Right," she said, feeling crushed. "Thanks anyway."

"But I have an idea," he said, perking up. "There's a special library at the private college with a lot of history about Triton Bay. Old books, original documents. My brother told me about it. Maybe we can do some research."

"That's so nerdy," she said, nudging him. "And so awesome at the same time."

"Totally is," he said with a thumbs-up.

She bit her lip. "Maybe we can find out more about the sea witch—she said her name was Ursula—and why she wants that trident so badly. I don't trust her. Not one bit."

He nodded. "And maybe we can find a way to stop this fish transformation from happening to you. I mean, I do love fish and all, but you make a pretty great human—"

Suddenly, the wind whipped up. A bolt of lightning struck the sea. It flashed with bright emerald light—*unnatural* light. Shelly waited for the deep rumble of thunder that always accompanied lightning. But instead, *cackling* rose from the waves. The laughter grew louder.

"Did you hear that?" Enrique said, casting his gaze out to the ocean. "What was that?"

Shelly swallowed hard against the sick feeling in her stomach. "That's the sea witch. She must have been listening to us."

They backed away from the water. The laughter died down, drifting away. But it had been unmistakable. And for the first time, Shelly had a witness. That meant something important.

She wasn't dreaming.

This was real.

"We have to do something," Enrique said, looking afraid.

"Yeah." Shelly studied her hands. "And whatever we do, we have to act fast."

15
HOOK, LINE, AND SINKER

"You get it?" Shelly asked Enrique as he appeared by the bike rack at the aquarium the next morning.

Feeling jittery and scared, she had raced as fast as she could to meet Enrique. When she'd woken up that morning, she'd noticed her skin had started to take on a greenish sheen. Scales had also started to appear on her arms, delicate and smooth like those of a fish. She wore long sleeves to hide them and kept them pulled down over her hands. She didn't have much time. She felt tense. If Enrique had failed at what he'd set out to do, she didn't know what else they could try.

But he winked at her. "Mission accomplished," he said

with a grin, pulling the card out of his back pocket. He handed it over. The ID card showed the pimply face of his brother, Miguel. Uneven bangs flopped into his brown eyes. STUDENT was printed over the crest for Triton Bay College, which featured a trident and a mermaid. "It's our ticket into the science library at the college, with the special Triton Bay archives," Enrique went on. "But we need to hurry before my brother notices I took it."

"Wait, you didn't tell him?" asked Shelly.

"Uh, that I needed to borrow it for my friend who's turning into a fish because she made a bad deal with a sea witch? Figured the less he knew, the better."

Shelly smiled. "Point taken."

"Look, he's working here for a few more hours. So the sooner we get back, the better."

"Then what are we waiting for? Let's go!" They got on their bikes, and Enrique took off. Shelly was about to pedal after him when two other figures on bikes appeared in the distance, careering down the path. A minute later, they skidded to a halt next to her, kicking up sand. Shelly stared in shock.

"Attina? Alana? What're you doing here?" she asked.

The twins exchanged conspiratorial glances.

"Well, you've been acting so weird lately," Alana said with a smirk. "Like how you ran into the locker room all freaked out after the last race. And Kendall said something, too."

"Yeah, about you cheating," Attina added. "Oh, and that maybe you're turning into a fish."

"Yeah, she told us about the webbing on your hands. Which would explain your super swim powers," Alana added. "It doesn't take a marine biologist to put it together. I mean, something has to be going on, right?"

"So we decided to follow you," Attina said, sharing a guilty look with her twin sister. "I mean, we were worried about you. You're our friend, right?"

"But . . . w-what about Kendall?" Shelly stammered. "She hates me now."

Attina rolled her eyes and sighed deeply. "Look, we never liked her that much, either. You're not the only one she bullies and orders around, you know?"

"And we're sick of it." Alana nodded.

"Plus, we're your friends," Attina said. "Friends help friends."

Enrique circled back around, skidding up on his bike. He grinned when he saw Shelly with her friends. "Oh, so this is the holdup?" he asked.

The twins grinned and batted their eyelashes at him.

Shelly felt a surge of gratitude. "My *friends* . . . they came to help us."

"The more, the merrier," he said. "We need all the help we can get."

* * *

Triton Bay College was located across the bay from the aquarium, perched on a sheer cliff overlooking the water. Waves swelled up against the steep, rocky incline. Shelly got dizzy just looking down over the side. They parked their bikes, then circled up to brief Attina and Alana on the wild events. "An actual sea witch?" Attina said. "Like in the old stories?"

"Yup, the old stories aren't just stories," Shelly said, pulling off her scarf to show them her gills. "Turns out they're real."

The twins stared in shock, but their shock turned to fascination.

"Wow, that is so *cool*," Alana said. "This is way exciting. Beats swim practice."

College students milled around campus, clutching bags stuffed with books and laptops, while seagulls and pelicans swooped overhead, diving past the cliff to the sea in search of food. The college was famous for its marine biology department. Shelly had always dreamed of going there when she got older. Feeling a stab of anxiety, she pulled her sleeves down farther. Never in a million years had she imagined that her first trip to the science library would be . . . like this.

Enrique glanced around to make sure nobody was watching. The students were too busy rushing to class to notice a few kids in hoodies who looked way too young to be enrolled there. They hurried across campus to the science library, a modern and sleek two-story building.

Shelly turned to Attina and Alana. "You two wait out here and keep watch, okay?"

"Text us if anybody gets suspicious," Enrique added. "Or if you spot my brother. Hopefully he won't notice that I swiped his ID card and come looking for me."

"We're on it!" the twins said together, settling on a

nearby bench. They pulled books from their backpacks and tried to blend in with the students around them.

Satisfied that their lookouts were in place, Enrique swiped his brother's ID through the scanner on the door. Shelly glanced out at the ocean, where it looked like a storm was brewing. She held her breath, praying the ID card worked. "Come on, unlock," she said in a low voice, "before Ursula catches on to what we're doing. She won't like it."

After what seemed like an eternity, the scanner finally beeped and turned green.

The door unlocked with a click.

Enrique glanced back at the ocean. "Yeah, that storm doesn't look natural."

"It's her," Shelly said ominously.

"Let's hurry." Enrique yanked the door open, and they slipped inside. The artificial cold of air-conditioning hit them. The corridor was well lit, but that made it worse. They weren't supposed to be in there.

"This way," Enrique said, taking her hand. Her scaly green skin was sensitive. A shiver ran up her spine at his touch. He pulled her down the hallway. Signs on the wall directed them toward the archives. They reached a door printed with a sign that read:

RESTRICTED

COLLEGE STUDENTS & STAFF ONLY

Shelly felt a jolt when she read it. She glanced down the hallway, but it was deserted.

"Here goes nothing," Enrique said, swiping his brother's ID in the scanner.

It unlocked with a beep and admitted them into the library. They slipped inside, hurrying past the check-in desk before anyone could ask for IDs. Fortunately, the librarian was too busy checking in books to notice. The library was lit with pools of light spilling down from chandeliers overhead. Bay windows spanned the entire wall, overlooking the sea. It was a stunning room built from old wood paneling and filled with rows of shelves, stacked to the ceiling with books.

A few students, absorbed in research, huddled over

their laptops at desks that were piled high with messy stacks of books. A general hush seemed to envelop the room.

It was eerie. Just the *tap-tap-tap* of fingers hitting keyboards.

"Hurry up. Come with me," Enrique said, pulling her toward the back of the library.

They wound their way down rows and rows of shelves. The farther back they went, the dimmer the light grew and the dustier the stacks became. Shelly sneezed twice in quick succession. That area of the library looked like it got little traffic, like nobody had touched the shelves in ages. Enrique came to a halt in front of another door marked by a bronze placard:

TRITON BAY HISTORICAL ARCHIVES

"This is it," Enrique said, swiping the ID card in the scanner.

The door beeped and unlocked. The lights inside were off, but the second they entered, a sensor triggered them to flicker on. Shelly felt a tickle in her nose and the urge to sneeze again. This room smelled even more like dust and decaying paper. It smelled *ancient*. The books in there appeared far older than the books in the main library. Tables were positioned around the room, displaying under thick glass books that featured old maps of Triton Bay. She ran her fingers over the glass, taking in the beautiful images. They looked hand-drawn and -inked.

She followed Enrique over to a bank of computers labeled DIGITAL ARCHIVES. The prompt demanded a username and password. Shelly frowned at the blinking cursor. "How're we going to log in?"

Enrique arched his eyebrow, then sat down at the computer. His fingers flew over the keyboard. He typed in his brother's first initial and last name, then entered a password.

"Here goes nothing," he said, hitting RETURN.

They both held their breath.

A second later, the password screen dissolved, revealing a search prompt.

She looked at him, impressed. "You can hack into a computer?"

"Ha, I wish!" he said with a smirk. "Miguel uses the same password for everything."

"Brothers," she said with a nod. "Can't live with 'em, can't live without 'em."

They turned their attention to the monitor. Enrique typed in some search terms—*sea witch, Triton Bay, myth, sailors*. The search icon spun. A few seconds later, results flooded the screen, spanning down the monitor. Shelly scanned them quickly. Her heart lurched when she saw the title of one of the archived documents:

THE SEA WITCH AND THE TRIDENT

"Click on that one," she said, pointing to it. Enrique did.

It appeared to be an old Triton Bay fairy tale. They both scanned the story, reading the flowing handwritten text that had been archived in the online database. Shelly read it aloud.

" 'Once upon a time, a powerful trident belonged to King Triton. It granted him the power to control the ocean and all the creatures in it. Whoever possessed the trident would automatically become the most powerful creature in the sea and could also wreak havoc on the world above if they so chose. That's why the sea witch would do anything to get it. One night, she tried to kill King Triton and take the trident from him. But he vanquished her in a great sea battle, diminishing her power. The king knew that the sea witch couldn't be trusted, so he used the trident to place a powerful spell on her that confined her to Triton Bay. Thus, the bay became her prison, where she would live out the rest of her days.'"

"There we have it," said Enrique.

Shelly nodded at the monitor. "Look, there's more."

Enrique read: "'But the king was still unsatisfied. He put a spell on the trident to protect it from falling into the wrong hands and hid it somewhere safe. According to the legends, nobody knew exactly where it was hidden.'"

"Until now," Shelly said, looking up from the computer.

Enrique thought for a moment. "It makes sense, right? The sea witch can't leave the bay. The aquarium is on dry land. So she can't get the trident."

"Hiding the trident in plain sight is perfect camouflage," Shelly said.

"Yup, it's brilliant," he agreed. "Everyone just thinks it's a fake aquarium prop."

"So is this why the sea witch wants the trident?" she said, tapping the screen. "To break the curse and escape from the bay?"

"Maybe, but it could be more sinister than that." He pointed to a line in the story. "If she gets the trident, then she'll be able to control the ocean and all the creatures in it. Think about what the sea witch could do with that kind of power. You said yourself you don't trust her."

"You're right. It could be devastating. . . ." Her voice trailed off. The words made them both feel afraid. She rolled up her sleeves, revealing her silvery-green scales. "But what am I supposed to do? I'm turning into a fish. This is the only way to get her to reverse the curse."

Enrique looked uneasy. Suddenly, the lights flickered. They both looked around. The wind whipped up outside the windows, and lightning strobed in the sky, bolting down and striking the sea. The lights in the library flickered again, as if they'd go out at any moment.

Shelly's phone went off, making them both jump. She pulled it out and showed Enrique:

NEW MESSAGE

FROM: *ATTINA*

THIS STORM IS GETTING WORSE! THERE'S SOMETHING STRANGE GLOWING IN THE WATER! PLEASE HURRY!!!

"This doesn't sound good," Shelly muttered softly. With trepidation, she approached the window and pressed her hands to the glass. Below their cliffside perch, the waves in the bay churned and surged unnaturally. Thick gray clouds swirled and gathered overhead, pulsing with lightning. One bolt struck the water with a brilliant flash. The lights in the room kept flickering.

Suddenly, something smacked the glass right by her head.

16
NIGHT DIP

Shelly leaped back from the window.

Her heart thudded against her chest like a drum while her breathing sped up, making her gills flare under her scarf. The object bounced off the glass. It was a plastic cup.

Just like the one she had thrown in the ocean.

More plastic cups, bottles, and straws started pelting the glass. The storm wasn't natural—it was raining plastic trash all over the campus. How was that possible? *Ursula*.

Feeling another jolt of fear, Shelly backed away from the trash pelting the window. Then another lightning bolt pulsed in the sky, illuminating Triton Bay. Instead of thunder, cackling laughter rang out. A flicker surged through the library, sparking and shorting out the computer monitor. The screen went dark. Then, one by one, the lights in the archives blinked out.

Shelly shook Enrique. "It's Ursula—she's coming for us!"

"Hurry, let's get out of here," Enrique said, grabbing her hand and pulling her toward the door. Outside, the whole library was dark. All the lights had shorted out from the storm.

They ran through the dark stacks, dodging the shelves as if they were navigating an obstacle course. More lightning pulsed outside, strobe lighting the library, but instead of the clap of thunder, cackling laughter rang out over the bay again. Suddenly, books starting crashing off the shelves, pelting their heads. They tried to dodge them and ran faster. When they reached the entrance, Shelly glanced back at the library. It was empty. That scared Shelly almost more than anything else, but before she could linger on it any longer, Enrique grabbed her hand and pulled her through the door. They dashed down the hall, running full speed, and emerged outside.

"There you are!" Attina said, running up to them.

Alana was right on her heels. They both looked afraid.

Instantly, the storm began to recede, the clouds withdrawing and vanishing.

"How is this possible?" Alana asked, her face drained of color.

"Yeah, it was raining *plastic*," Attina added with a shudder. "And were those glowing eyes in the ocean?"

"Yes. It's her. It's Ursula," Shelly said. "She didn't want us to find that story."

"You're right," Enrique agreed with a frightened expression. "She wants that trident—no, she *needs* that trident. It's the only way she can break her curse and escape from the bay."

"And she's willing to do anything to get it," Shelly said, her stomach knotting up.

Alana's eyes shifted to her and held her gaze. "And you're her only hope of getting it."

"And if she gets it . . ." began Attina. Her words hung in the air. They all knew how dangerous the sea witch would become if she escaped from her watery prison with the power of the whole ocean behind her. Shelly bit her lower lip. She inhaled and felt her gills flare.

"But if I don't help the sea witch, then I'll turn into a fish. *Forever*," she said.

They looked at one another for a long, deep moment. Enrique clasped Shelly's hand. She glanced down at the scaly skin that peeked out from under her sleeve. It glinted like silver in the dwindling daylight. "We'll help you," Enrique said. "Just tell us what you need us to do."

"Listen, it's getting too dangerous," said Shelly, wheeling on her friends. "I'll text you if I need help. But I think you should all head home to safety. I'll be okay. Promise. I couldn't bear anything bad happening to any of you. And thank you for your help. It means a lot. Really."

Reluctantly, the twins nodded and biked away, leaving Shelly alone with Enrique.

When she tried to tell him to leave, too, he said, "You're not doing this alone."

"Resistance is futile?" she replied.

"See, you are a true nerd," he said with a glint in his eye.

NIGHT DIP

* * *

Shelly laid her bike on the beach, then followed Enrique down a long pier that stretched out over the black water. They had to formulate a plan for how to deal with the sea witch. Shelly heard the sloshing of waves and tasted the briny tang of salt water on her tongue. It felt like walking out to the edge of the universe. The dark ocean seemed to have no end.

"You sure this is safe?" she said, glancing off the pier. The salt turned acrid on her tongue. Unlike a lot of kids, Shelly had never been afraid of the ocean or the mysterious creatures that lay beneath the surface. But that had all changed. Each wave that sloshed against the pier made her jump as she imagined black tentacles shooting out at her from the depths.

"We're outside Triton Bay," Enrique said with a lopsided smile. "The sea witch can't leave the bay, remember? I come out here sometimes when I need to think or be alone. Also, the views are incredible." He pointed back toward the lights of their little seaside town.

Just a few days before, their town had seemed idyllic

and safe, but now Shelly knew a darker truth. Their town was haunted by an evil, malevolent presence imprisoned in the bay.

"Think your bro noticed that we took his ID?" she asked, following him down to the edge of the pier. They'd returned it to his backpack before biking there.

"I doubt it," Enrique said. "He was too busy working with the dolphin trainers."

She glanced down at her hands clad in the gloves. "I never should have tried to change myself. It was a huge mistake."

"Why'd you do it?" he asked thoughtfully.

"When I first switched schools, I didn't have any friends. And *no friends* is the worst. But then I finally made some. And I guess I was afraid that if I didn't win my race at the next swim meet, then I'd lose them."

"That's why you made your wish?"

"Yeah, it sounds silly now, but I wanted to impress Kendall. Like I said, huge mistake."

He shot her a sympathetic look and shook his head sadly. "But that's not a real friend," he said. "Real friends should like you exactly the way you are."

Tears pricked her eyes. "Yeah, I learned that the hard way. It all backfired anyway. Winning my race only made Kendall hate me more. It's all been such a disaster."

Though, at least Attina and Alana had been there for her today. She hadn't lost everything.

"Well, I'm your friend."

She could tell he meant it, even in her freaky, fishy cursed state.

Suddenly, back over Triton Bay, a bolt of green lightning streaked through the sky and struck the ocean—and this time she saw an image in the flash. It was Enrique—slowly shrinking and starting to turn into one of those strange, pathetic creatures trapped in Ursula's lair.

Shelly jerked her head away. The image was a clear warning from the sea witch not to double-cross her. And it had also signaled something else—something far worse.

As she'd feared, she wasn't the only one in danger anymore.

Enrique was, too.

"Come on, let's turn back," she said, feeling cold. Nothing felt safe anymore.

"So, what's the plan then?" he asked, seeing the

frightened look in her eyes as they headed back to the beach.

"Tomorrow," she said, knowing that she didn't have a choice anymore. She couldn't let that horrible fate befall Enrique. They had to get the trident. There was no way around it. "Meet at the aquarium after sunset," she told him, eyes narrowing. "And we'll take the trident."

17

THE TRIDENT

The spare security card had a silver key ring attached to a yellow-and-blue foam flounder.

Shelly had stolen it from a drawer in her mother's home office the night before, and now, with Enrique by her side, she swiped the security card, then slid the key into the lock. The new security system frightened her. Her father had it installed after a recent series of strange burglary attempts. The police thought it had been local teens, but Shelly wondered if it was something far more insidious—*Ursula*. What if they were wrong and she *could* leave the bay? The foam flounder bopped around, and she held her breath, then twisted. The bolts turned and released, admitting them into the dark aquarium.

Enrique gave her a thumbs-up. "Nice work."

They slipped through the side entrance and followed the corridor down the main hall. The main lights were out, but the exhibits were still lit with their signature blue-green light that cast eerie shadows through the cavernous space. The aquarium felt totally different after hours, when the tourists had cleared out, leaving their sticky residue behind. No kids played tag, careering around the exhibits, or pressed their noses to the glass. No parents chased them, looking exhausted. Instead, it was quiet and foreboding. Not even staff were there. The sea witch was watching; she'd know if they failed. They couldn't let that happen.

Suddenly, Shelly felt short of breath, like her lungs couldn't get enough oxygen. Enrique glanced back at her in alarm. He noticed her struggling to keep up. "What's wrong?" he asked.

"I'm . . . having a hard time . . . breathing," she managed, still gasping for air. Her lungs were screaming at her. "It feels like my lungs suddenly . . . aren't working."

He pulled her toward the nearest tank. "Hurry, over here! I have an idea."

"What . . . do you mean?" she gasped. "Where are you taking me?"

"Maybe it's the gills," he said, leading her to a small tank and removing the top. "Fish can't breathe out of water, remember? And you're turning into . . ."

"A fish," she said, recalling zombie Mr. Bubbles saying, *You're going to go belly-up!*

"Just try it," Enrique said, and she dunked her head into the tank on command.

As soon as the salt water hit her gills, it was like she could breathe again. Really breathe. Gradually, her lungs stopped screaming. She pulled her head out with a frightened expression.

Their eyes met. He held her gaze. "That means . . ."

"Not much time left," she finished in barely a whisper. Her eyes fell on the main exhibit that towered over the hall. The reef shark darted around the trident, coasting by the pirate ship.

Enrique followed her gaze. "How are we going to get it?"

"Superpowers, remember?" she said, stripping off her

scarf and gloves, revealing her hands, which were now more fish than human.

"It's really progressing, huh?" he said. "Your hands weren't like this yesterday."

She nodded. "Faster than before."

Her lungs constricted; she was gasping for oxygen. "Let's go," she said, pulling him toward the main exhibit into the staff-only area. "I need to hurry up and get into the tank, or I'm going to have trouble breathing again."

They hurried down an echoing stairwell into the bowels of the exhibit, where few got to go. There, it looked and felt industrial, and at night, almost sinister. The space behind the scenes consisted of metal scaffolding, rusty ladders, and other equipment. She led Enrique over to a ladder that ran up the side of the main exhibit. Light from the tank washed over them as they climbed up and onto the catwalk that spanned the tank. Shelly looked down at the rippling water, illuminated by its artificial light. There were sharks in the tank, but she wasn't really afraid.

"You know, something's been bothering me," Enrique said, shooting her a worried look. He balanced on the catwalk beside her, wobbling.

THE TRIDENT

"What's that?" Shelly unzipped her hoodie to reveal her wet suit beneath.

"It's almost like the sea witch knew this fish curse would help you get the trident for her. Because it's easy for you to swim into the tank. It's like this was part of her plan all along."

Shelly gulped. "Maybe you're right."

"She's evil—and wicked smart," he said with a shake of his head. "She tricked you."

Shelly handed him an oxygen mask and fins. "Here. Since you don't have superpowers like me and all."

He laughed, then pulled on the mask. She switched on the oxygen line. He gave her another thumbs-up. Then they clambered farther down the catwalk. It was slippery and narrow. She'd never swum inside the main exhibit. It was dangerous with sharks and other animals, not to mention the hazards of diving with an oxygen line. One needed to be a trained professional, but she might as well have been. They hovered over the pirate ship. She could just see it through the rippling water.

"Here goes nothing," she said, diving into the tank with a soft splash.

PART OF YOUR NIGHTMARE

Enrique followed, landing with a churn of bubbles beside her. He was clumsier in the water with all the gear, but she was practically a fish now.

She cut through the tank, diving toward the ship, past it and the faux treasure chest.

The trident stood before her, skewering the sand.

Enrique caught up. Without thinking, he reached out to grab the trident—but she batted his hand away just in time. A bolt of electricity shot out from the trident, nearly zapping him.

"Let me," she said, and somehow her voice rang out clear as day through the water.

He nodded.

Suddenly, warning voices sounded.

"Don't trust her—she lies!"

But then she looked down at her feet, which were fully turning into fins now, and over at Enrique, remembering the sea witch's threat to turn him into one of her writhing creatures. She had to reverse the curse. She had to help the sea witch.

She grasped the trident.

THE TRIDENT

Though it seemed to be wedged in the sand, at her touch it came loose with surprising ease.

No electric shocks zapped her.

Then, all at once, the barnacles fell away, revealing a gleaming, golden weapon.

She felt great power emanating from the ancient weapon, but also danger.

Suddenly, alarms sounded. Removing the trident must have triggered them. They had to get out of there before the police came. Enrique gave her a startled look. Together, they swam upward. But his oxygen line got snagged on the pirate ship—and came unplugged. He struggled to free himself, unable to breathe. Then, suddenly, the reef shark darted toward Shelly.

The shark looked agitated, too. Like something had gotten into him. An unnatural emerald light flashed in the shark's eyes. Part of the enchantment to protect the trident?

The shark cracked open its jaws and zeroed in on the trident.

Shelly tried to swim away to help get Enrique to the

surface, but the shark latched on to the trident with its huge jaws. It began to wrench it from her hand as she fought to drive it away. Meanwhile, Enrique struggled toward the surface, but Shelly feared he wouldn't make it without her help. She could let go of the trident and save Enrique—but then the curse would last forever.

She gripped the trident harder. *Please help me,* she thought.

Suddenly, she felt power emanate through the trident and explode in a blast of green light that blew the shark back through the water. But the shark recovered—and darted for Enrique.

Shelly pivoted and swam toward Enrique, snatching him just as the shark snapped at his torso and missed. But they weren't out of danger yet. The shark darted around to attack again.

Shelly felt something slip out of her pocket; it was the nautilus. It drifted to the bottom of the exhibit, where it settled in the sand next to the treasure chest. She started to swim for it, but the shark charged at them again. Without wasting another second, Shelly hooked her arm around Enrique and swam fast for the surface. She saw his eyes were closed. He needed oxygen right away. The shark was right on her heels and starting to close in on them.

Shelly tried to swim faster, but even with her fish abilities, Enrique and the trident were slowing her down. She kicked harder, feeling her fins claw against the water. Finally, she burst through the surface and up the ladder, dragging Enrique onto the catwalk with her last remaining strength. At that moment, the shark's open mouth broke the surface, missing his dangling leg by inches.

The trident clattered down on the catwalk with a metallic rattle.

The alarms continued blaring, along with the emergency lights flashing overhead.

Shelly turned her attention back toward Enrique. "Come on! Wake up!" she yelled, shaking Enrique. He had once saved her. She couldn't fail him.

He coughed, then flipped over and spat out salt water. He gasped for air and breathed deeply.

"Oh, thank the seven seas," Shelly said with a rush of relief. "You scared me!"

He coughed again. "Did you get it?" he asked.

"Yes. But us being here after hours must have triggered the alarms. We have to get out of here!"

She helped Enrique to his feet, and he staggered unsteadily on the catwalk.

While the alarms kept blaring, they hurried back to the entrance, but when they got there, the doors wouldn't open. Shelly tried the keys and the security card. Nothing worked.

"We're trapped. It must be a security measure," Enrique said. "It's probably alerting the authorities."

She swallowed hard. "Or my parents." Shelly felt their time ticking away. Her lungs screamed for oxygen now that she was out of the tank. It was getting worse fast. She couldn't risk getting trapped or caught by her parents. They didn't have much time left to take the trident to Ursula's lair.

Any second they'd be busted. And then it would be too late.

"What do we do?" she gasped. They couldn't escape the way they came in. It was getting harder for her to breathe by the second. Her mind felt sluggish. She clutched the trident tightly.

"What about the shell?" asked Enrique. "The one that takes you to Ursula's lair?"

"I dropped it in the exhibit, when the shark came after you."

They both turned to look. The shark was circling the shell. They couldn't risk going back into the tank—the shark would attack them again. And this time, they might not be so lucky. Shelly met Enrique's eyes. She could tell that they were both thinking the same thing.

What now?

18

LAST STRAW

The alarms continued to blare in the aquarium.

Shelly glanced over at Enrique; he looked afraid. Desperately, she tried to think of another way out—but they were trapped.

Cackling laughter tore through the aquarium, accompanied by the sea witch's voice.

"My dearie, don't fail me! Your time is almost up! Now, fork it over!"

Shelly saw a flash of Enrique again as a sea polyp. "No!" she yelled. That's when Shelly had a wild idea. She grabbed Enrique's hand while still clutching the trident with her other. She could feel power surging through the weapon. "To the sundeck! It's the only way out!"

PART OF YOUR NIGHTMARE

They ran the other way, bolted up the stairs, and emerged onto the sundeck. Wind whipped off the ocean. The dolphins circled in their exhibit. They knew something was wrong.

Overhead, a storm was brewing—and not just any storm—an unnatural storm. Bright lightning pulsed in the dark sky, lighting up the clouds, while the ocean grew turbulent. In the distance, Shelly saw the two yellow eyes of the sea eels blink open in the dark water. They swam in opposite directions. The sea witch was watching them.

"Come on," she said, leading Enrique to the catwalk over the open ocean. It was the same spot where she had littered, dropping the plastic cup at her friends' urging. It was also where the giant wave had snatched her.

I made a mistake by littering, she thought. *I'm sorry.*

She'd learned her lesson. More than learned it. Littering in the ocean was wrong. If only she'd done the right thing and hadn't bent to peer pressure, then none of this would be happening. She just hoped she still had time to make it right.

The waves sloshed up onto the catwalk, spritzing them with seawater. She tasted it on her tongue and breathed it into her lungs. She held the trident in her hand and peered into the dark ocean, filled with angry whitecaps. The wind whipped up, making the sea churn faster. Shelly could feel the power of the trident flowing through her body. She remembered what it had done to the shark.

"Hurry, dive in!" Enrique said, standing next to her on the catwalk. Rain and wind pelted his face and body. "Swim to her lair. Take her the trident. That's the only way to stop this."

Shelly wanted to . . . but something was stopping her. "No, it's too dangerous," she said. "I can't give her the trident."

Fear flashed in his eyes. "What do you mean? You don't have a choice!"

"Did you see what it did to the shark?" she replied while the wind whipped at her. "If we give the trident to Ursula, then she could use it to do bad things . . . terrible things to everyone."

Enrique glanced out over Triton Bay—the only place they'd ever called home, with all the people who lived there—then met Shelly's gaze. He looked grim. "You're right . . . but if you don't do it, then there's no way to reverse the curse. You'll turn into a fish for good."

Fear tore through Shelly. The thought of turning into a fish forever, of leaving her family and friends, terrified her and made her heart ache. But if she gave the trident to the sea witch, then the witch would have the power to hurt everybody she loved—her mom and dad; Dawson; Enrique and his brother, Miguel; Mr. Aquino; Attina and Alana. Even Kendall and Judy Weisberg.

She couldn't let that happen. She'd made a mistake before—she'd done the wrong thing by littering in the ocean, by letting other people make decisions for her—but now she could make a better choice, even if it cost her everything.

This was her chance to make it right.

Shelly stepped down from the catwalk and backed away from the water, trident in hand.

"I can't give it to her!" she yelled over the wind and rain. "I have to do the right thing and protect Triton Bay, like my parents. I was selfish before. I can't make that same mistake again."

Enrique met her eyes and held her gaze once again.

LAST STRAW

He looked troubled, but he managed a weak smile. Shelly could see that he knew she was right, even if it cost him something important, too.

"I always knew you were special—" he started.

But then a black tentacle shot out of the ocean and wrapped around his chest. His eyes widened with fear, and then the tentacle yanked him off the catwalk and dragged him into the ocean.

Before he vanished beneath the waves, he locked eyes with Shelly and yelped.

And then he was gone.

19
FISH OUT OF WATER

Shelly reached out for Enrique, but she was too late.

The tentacle had jerked him underwater. *Ursula.*

Shelly dove after him. She had to save him. As she hit the water, her gills pulled it in, drinking it up gratefully. Adrenaline pumped through her veins while her heart hammered in her chest. The image of Enrique turning into a poor unfortunate soul flashed through her head.

She couldn't let the sea witch hurt her friend. She was the one who had made the mistake. Enrique was just trying to help. Through the murky water, she could make out two glowing yellow eyes—the sea eels. She couldn't let them out of her sight. With any luck, they'd lead her right to Ursula's lair. She just hoped she wasn't too late to save Enrique.

Clutching the trident, she swam fast after the sea eels, plunging deeper and deeper into the frigid water. Her webbed hands and feet propelled her while her gills processed the oxygen and kept her breathing. Her brain kept replaying Enrique being seized by the black tentacle and whipped underwater. He wasn't like her. He couldn't breathe down there.

Finally, after what seemed like an eternity, she spotted the entrance to Ursula's lair: the bony exoskeleton of some sort of mammoth sea creature with a gaping mouth full of sharp teeth.

She swam through the entrance, ignoring the protests of those eerie voices again.

"Don't give her the trident!" they wailed. *"She'll become too powerful!"*

Something grabbed her legs, but Shelly kicked it away and kept swimming. "I'm sorry," she whispered, not knowing who she was speaking to, or if there was even anyone there. "I have to save my friend."

When she emerged in the shadowy lair, her eyes became fixed on the crystal ball. Enrique was collapsed inside of it. At first, she was worried that he was dead. He wasn't moving at all.

She swam over to the crystal ball and pounded on the outside. The glass was too strong. She couldn't crack it open, nor did she want to. The crystal ball was filled with air, not water.

"Enrique, wake up!" She pounded on the glass harder. "Don't die on me!"

He lay there, not breathing.

But then his chest moved slightly.

He was starting to breathe again.

But he was trapped—a prisoner.

"Ursula, I'm here!" Shelly yelled. She whipped around, trying to locate the sea witch. "I did what you wanted. I got the trident for you! Now come and get it—and keep your promise."

She held up the ancient weapon, feeling a bolt of electricity run down it. The trident was infused with *great* power, *ancient* power, *dangerous* power. But Shelly had to save her friend.

PART OF YOUR NIGHTMARE

This was the only way.

Slowly, a huge form rose out of the shadows and slunk into the lair, illuminated by the light from the crystal ball. The sea witch finally revealed herself in her full glory. Her head and torso were human, but her lower body was the tentacles of a black octopus. They undulated around her, giving her a menacing appearance. She grinned, displaying all her glittering teeth. Her lips were glossy with bloodred lipstick, and she had spiky white hair. "My dear, you succeeded," she said with a cackle. "I had a feeling you had it in you."

Shelly plunged the trident into the sand in front of the sea witch. "There, it's all yours! Just like you wanted. Now take it—and keep your promise to me. Change me back, and let my friend go! He doesn't have anything to do with this. He's innocent!"

Ursula grinned, snatching the trident. As soon as her clawed hand touched the weapon, a bolt of electricity shot down her arm and through her body. Her eyes glowed with yellow light while electrical zaps fizzled through her.

She cackled with glee. "The protection spell is broken! Now it's mine—all mine!"

The ocean current grew stronger, churning through the lair. Shelly had to brace herself against it. Bolts of electricity flickered, running down the length of the golden trident.

"Hurry!" Shelly yelled. "Reverse the curse! And let my friend go!"

Ursula aimed the trident at her. "As you wish, my dear!"

A blast of electricity shot out of the forked end and hit Shelly square in the chest. She felt pain surge through her entire body, then recede. A great feeling of relief swept through her.

The sea witch had kept her promise.

Shelly looked down at her hands, waiting for the spell to take effect. But they remained fins. Her gills were still there. She could feel them flaring and sucking in the water. Then something horrible happened. She felt her legs seal together, fully becoming a tail.

Ursula peered at her with a fierce grin, an eel wrapped around each arm. "You belong to me now!" she cackled at Shelly, waving the trident in her hand.

"But we had a deal," Shelly managed to say. Her voice came out shrill.

Ursula laughed heartily, looking down on her with pity. The whites of her eyes shone in the darkness. "Oh, my dear, it's not a deal unless you sign a contract. Otherwise, it's up for negotiation."

"What do you mean?" Shelly sputtered. Her voice sounded like Mr. Bubbles's.

"No contract—no deal."

"You're a liar! You tricked me!"

"Oh, my dear, it's not a lie—it's just sea business," Ursula said with a wink. She unfurled the contract. Shelly's signature glinted in gold. "You're the fastest swimmer now . . . *forever.*"

Shelly opened her mouth to reply, but nothing came out.

The last thing she remembered was Ursula holding up the trident and grinning down at her. "Oh, don't worry, my dear," Ursula said in a smug voice. "You did prove your usefulness."

Shelly wanted to scream, but only bubbles came out.

"I've got something very special in mind for you," Ursula said.

TRITON BAY TRIBUNE

NEW AQUARIUM EXHIBIT OPENS IN LOVING MEMORY OF SHELLY ANDERSON

It's been six months since local middle schooler Shelly Anderson went missing on the day of the aquarium break-in. The reason for her disappearance remains a mystery, though the police believe the two events must be connected.

MISSING signs, weather-beaten and yellowing, can still be seen posted to telephone poles and buildings throughout Triton Bay. Even the promise of a $10,000 reward hasn't turned up any leads on Shelly Anderson's whereabouts.

This week, her disappearance was officially filed in the state of California as a cold case.

But somehow, in all this, Shelly's family's aquarium has endured, perched above the ocean like a castle. Today a special occasion drew in a crowd.

Her parents, the owners of the aquarium, stood before the main exhibit with their young son, Dawson. They all clutched an oversize pair of scissors. Behind them, a turquoise ribbon with a big knotted bow stretched across the front of the massive tank, which was draped with a curtain.

While today was a day of remembrance for their missing daughter, it was also a celebration of what's in store.

"Welcome to the unveiling of our newly refurbished main attraction," Mr. Anderson said with a smile to the crowd. He gave his wife's hand a gentle squeeze.

Ms. Anderson spoke next. "While we are saddened over the disappearance of our daughter, we remain hopeful that she will return one day."

"An anonymous donor funded

this new exhibit," said Mr. Anderson. "Today, we dedicate it to Shelly. We love you, honey. We'll always love you. We hope you come home."

The somber crowd cheered. The emotion in the room was palpable. Some of the local schoolgirls, presumably friends of Shelly's, cried and dabbed at their eyes with tissues.

One girl, Kendall Terran, later stated, "She was my very *best* friend." After sobbing for several seconds, she asked, "You got that? Like hashtag BFF. By the way, I'm also the captain of the swim team."

Meanwhile, another friend, a boy named Enrique, stood with his older brother. Upon being questioned, he couldn't remember much from that fateful night. He was discovered washed up on the beach. It was almost like his memory was stolen.

He just knows his friend is gone.

"Without further ado . . ." Mr. Anderson said, and then together, as a family, they cut the ribbon.

The curtain fell away.

Behind them, in the exhibit, a bronze statue of Shelly stood where the trident once was. A small green fish darted around the statue's face, then swam up to the glass.

The fish bumped up against the glass, drawing the attention of the boy, Dawson.

He clutched a curious spiral seashell, a keepsake, he stated, that once belonged to Shelly. They found it at the bottom of the exhibit the day she went missing. He pressed his face to the thick glass, peering at the fish.

"Hey, fishy, want to come home with me and live in my aquarium?" he said. "Mommy, I found a new pet!"

Ms. Anderson nodded, and the family held each other. The ceremony was a peaceful one, ending with guests laying flowers against the glass as another day in Triton Bay came to a serene close.

ACKNOWLEDGMENTS

This book is a collaboration as much as anything. It wouldn't be here without Eric Geron. You're the best editor any writer could hope for—and a fantastic human. Thrilled we got to work together. And on something *creepy*. Thanks for coming up with this chilling book series and for approaching me to author it. Thanks always to my book agent, Deborah Schneider, for being in my corner; the Studios of Key West for awarding me a writing residency, where I broke many of the ideas that appear in this book and channeled inspiration from the ocean; and the Vermont Studio Center and my friend Joj for bringing me to Provence, where I revised these pages. I also want to thank my grandfather Robert

Rogers, who consulted with Walt Disney on the music for *Fantasia* and other projects. I know you'd be so proud of me. Last, special thanks to my parents for taking me to see *Bambi*, my first movie, and inspiring a lifelong affinity for Disney. And yes, I've always liked the Disney villains best. Writing this book was a wish my heart made as a kid who loved scary books. I hope you enjoy this delightfully frightening series, dear reader.